Dos

Dear Shazia ~
Thank you for all of your
support and may all your work
be blessed - it is so important!
Love,
Chiara

Chiara Spadea

"Tell a story... sometimes it is much more interesting to just give the beginning of a story and not finish it. Get it started and let it go, let it go where people want it to go. It is more interesting to not give the story a beginning, middle and an end...it's confining...just leave it open... suggest..."

A Kiedis
Stadium Arcadium

TABLE OF CONTENTS

ABOUT THE AUTHOR

A believer, a mother, a sportswoman, a carer, a waternymph..a writer, a reader, a traveller, a global nomad. This best describes the author and the depth behind the stories created. Hailing from a global 'growing up' the author brings hard hitting stories that are softened by the characters and the humanness of the relationships formed. She draws on a life of fluidity in terms of environment and her immigrant background has gifted her the ability to observe the world through many lenses and reflect the modern world in terms of identity and integrity.

CHAPTER ONE

I hope they are not watching this... last time was violent, they were terrified... Fuck I wish I could just disappear. He makes no sense when he is like this, he just wants a fix and nothing I do or say will make it appear, so taking his beating is twice as bad because I never know when it will stop. My head is bleeding now... no wonder we have to hide in the doorframes when there is an earthquake they really are that fucking solid...

That is all that was running through my head as I lift my arm up again to defend myself from another blow. My partner was a junkie now, a full-fledged junkie. He is a full-fledged junkie without a fix to be found and raging. Things didn't start out like this, in fact we were the best of friends and born to be together but now he is lost to me and the person I thought I would grow old with is a monster. He came home from his job today and was pheening badly. His manager had told him he was on his last warning because she caught him sleeping in the staff room when he should have been defrosting the massive freezers for their annual clean. He always thought her job should have been his and resented her, so here we are now. He wants a fix, he has no fix, he is out of cash and can't get a fix, so what to do... beat the living shit out of his 'soul mate'; crash all my hopes of living a decent loved existence, diminish any love and respect me and his two little gifts had for him. Nah, they are not watching this, surely Lily has taken Jason into her room and is reading him a story like she did last time. ..

"You fat fucking bitch, you worthless whore! You ruined my life, I wasted all of the best years of my life with you and what have you given me?!! Just more mouths to feed, just permission for the rest of the world to shit all over me because they know I have a 'lovely girlfriend and two kids' to feed!"

He is just shouting all that he can now but he forgets I've heard it all before so I don't respond. Maybe my tactic needs to change though because he is hitting me harder and now he has a clump of my hair and is looking around for something. Unlucky for me he finds Jason's leather belt he left in the family room when he came home after school. Brody's face lights up at the prospect of the power the belt wields and now I am scared, now I know damage will be done and I will not be able to get up tomorrow or look after my babies.

He wants blood, it's written on his face. Oh please God save me from this, please do not let me die.

Whip! I swear it has ripped my shirt and torn a piece of flesh from my back.

Saalaap that hit the back of my neck and almost wound its harsh leather around my neck like a noose, I reach up and pull the belt away and try to grab it off him; now I am screaming. But the screams are coming from the anger surging inside me, not the pain, the pain is dull but the anger is real, it throbs and courses through my body. This anger expands and I have never felt such a surge to attack. I always had issues with my anger, namely that I always held it in and never expressed it or directed it at the person who caused it, but tonight it feels different. The thought of my lovely little Lily sitting in her room, covering up her fear with a sweet sounding story so her little brother will forget about the hellish torrent whirling outside their door. The fact the man causing me such harm is worthless and has become a down trodden misery compared to what he was and the recognition that all the promises, hope and love that existed once upon a time was all a fucking fairy tale, a load of shit that I held on to as I had nothing and no one else in the world; it was all so clear now, I messed up, I misjudged,

I got it wrong and now I wasn't the only one that would pay the price. Enough! I knew I could not contain the anger inside me now, I knew that my own primal defences where not going to be suppressed this time. This thing inflicting pain upon me was going to pay dearly now, no way was I going to take any more of this shit.

I reached out and clawed his leg so he pushed my head down farther and *slap* another whip across the back for me. I grabbed the hand that had the belt with one hand and tried to grab the hand holding my hair with the other. Once I had them I started pushing him with all my strength, trying to get him to lose his balance or let go of something. It worked and he let go of my hair so I lifted my head up and looked at him in the face. I stared into his eyes and started screaming at him to stop. The belt came flying back across my body and got me on the side, pain is shooting through my ribs and back but I know if I stop I will not survive this night. I launch a full on body attack; I know I have to get that belt off him. Every chance he gets he rains down blow after blow, but I am not backing down now. It's either him or me but someone will die tonight. I let go of him and lunge at him, I grabbed his balls and twist them as hard as I can while he delivers a splendid slap of the belt across my back again. Now his screams fill my ears and for a split second natural compassion messes with my mind and my vice on his balls loosens just enough for him to stop screaming. He is squirming, his own primal fears of death to his manhood filled him with an animalistic fight and he pulled my leg out from under me and we tumbled, finally crashing down, straight through the coffee table; wood splinters and my head sharply jolted back.

We both laid still, the shock of the intensity of our anger meeting somewhere between our bodies and freezing time and silencing the world. Somehow we are staring in each other's eyes, the years between us are playing out in front of us like a drive-in film, my eye clouds up with blood and as I look at him through my literal red mist I see what a despot he has become, he looks old, skinny and worn out, it's like life has beaten him and won. The anger I had inside was matched evenly with his own and through our stare we communicated an odd understanding, we realised that life had played us out, we were existing on fumes, as the collective we no longer existed and no future lay ahead for us. Something deep down inside, something that had felt hurt and was now irreparable began to come forth from my bruised lips.

"Look at the state of us, look what you did to me, look what you did to yourself. There is nothing left for us, nothing for us to do now but either kill each other or walk away. I am going to let go of you and walk away. The blood you see is blood on your hands but blood I will have to explain to the kids and the people out there who have known for the last five years that I was too good for you, that I gave you way too many chances. I don't want to be everyone's sympathy patch anymore, I don't want to be anything for you anymore. I am going to let go of you and let you fuck off and get your fix from some dark, dingy hole that only you have had the misery of knowing, but do not come back, do not come home anymore. I am a human not a dog, you cannot beat me like this and feel no repercussion. You will pay tonight, you will pay dearly."

So I let him go and he immediately let go of his dignity and integrity. My head was so sore, my body ached so badly and I had lost track of how many lashes I had taken but pushed him off me and as I slowly stood up and squared my shoulders. I made myself big, looking down at him; trying to look like I was ready for anything, ready to take him out if need be when really I just wanted to crumple and cry.

He dropped the belt and eyes, still wide and soulless, sat up gingerly on the floor. Tears sprung to his eyes, his face almost melted into a stew of self-pity. "I'm sorry Soleil, I'm so so sorry."

"I don't give fuck this time Brody, your eyes say it all, you are dead inside, we are dead! This is done, I am done. Get out! If you have any integrity left in your pathetic body get the fuck out of here and never come back. I know you will fuck off get fixed up and come home begging for me to forgive and forget. But I'm done you bastard, you go get that fix, make it a good one, make it so rich and nice that you fucking die. I feel nothing for you now. You won't miss your kids you shit, you probably don't even know what color your son's eyes are these days."

He jerked his head up to look at me with his blackened pits and hollow cheeks, a picture of Death almost looking surprised that I was telling it to go away, that I wasn't going to bend to Its will and take whatever It had in store.

"No, you cannot be without me, you know we are a pair, a unit, together we are stronger remember..." he whispered.

"One day you will kill me Brody, and I'm not on that journey with you anymore,"

"Soleil, you will always be part of me, I do this because you don't listen to me, you don't understand the pressure I feel when I look at you and the kids. That bitch at work today, she..."

"Shut up Brody, just shut up. Look at me, look what you have done to me. How can you deny what you see in my eyes? We are done, our life together is hell, you are not my friend anymore, you became my enemy the first time you injected that shit, you should have trusted in me that we would be ok, you should never have given up and let yourself be lost to that shit."

Deathboy looked forlorn and confused but I knew he had understood and was struggling to accept that his life was catching up with him.

"Look at me Brody, look what you have done to me, I am standing here by a miracle, you have hurt me, broken me and no one has ever beaten me like this and I swear no one ever will."

"You're right Soleil, no one ever will"

Out of nowhere he lunged and tackled me down to the ground; he looked like a lunatic and was almost wild with rage. He felt so much heavier and stronger like he had been possessed by a demon intent on my demise.

"You can go, I'll fucking send you there faster than you can blink bitch" he snarled as his hands found their way around my throat.

"If you think you can tell me I fucked this up and I am to blame you are wrong. You need me to breathe, you need me to live, you are nothing and never will be!"

His hands felt cold and darkness was coming over me, I didn't want to go but with all the struggling I was doing he seemed to get stronger and stronger. My anger welled up again but to no avail, I couldn't get his hands off me. How did it come to this? What would happen to my babies? No God please help me, why this? Please don't do this to my babies....

Swimming in the crystal clear water, I see fishes and sunlight pouring through the shallow waves. What a glorious place to be, swimming and smiling, Brody pointing excitedly to an eel as he magically unwinds from his hiding place. How did I get back here? This paradise, this glorious pool of eternity, bejewelled with colors so rich and alive that found no restriction in penetrating your skin and rejuvenating you with light.

My skin is tanned and taut; this is the trip we took to Mexico before Lily was born. What a trip, we were so in love, so passionate. We could hardly keep our hands off each other. We found a small hut by the beach and convinced the owner to go stay in our hotel so we could stay at his as he had a better view! We slept on the beach, drank tequila with the locals and loved every minute of every day we were together. The sun would blaze down on us and the pure white sand would stick to his muscular tanned frame and look like diamond flecks in his hair. He was gorgeous, everyone loved him and when he brought out his guitar and sang an old Spanish love song to me, I knew I was where I belonged. He was my world, swimming in the sea with him was like travelling to the moon, I trusted him completely and swam with him till we were exhausted, astounded by the fish and corals that came to life when the sun hit them. When we could no longer swim we would lie on the beach and bask in the glorious sunshine then with a renewed vigour we would fall into each other and challenge each other's passion time and time again. It was bliss, we were so happy but that one night... black clouds rolled over our piece of paradise and the wind ripped through the trees warning us that good times will end and happiness is futile... it got dark... its getting darker... I don't want to go! I have my babies now... I have real love, a place in this world.... Please let me get back to the light. I am struggling now but I feel like I am being held under water... my soul is screaming, it is not my time, how does it get so dark so quickly?! Keep to the light, the light that shone down, that lighted up the seas and made the fish look like firecrackers and the coral dance... Go to the light Soleil, love is not lost, it is there...

CHAPTER TWO

I came to and saw a blurry vision of Rodrigo kicking Brody in the side. He was screaming at him and cussing him telling him he was no man and he wished he had killed him sooner.

"Rodrigo, what is going on?! What happened? Where are Lily and Jason?" I barely whisper, my throat sore and crumpled.

"Fucking hell Soleil your alive, this asshole isn't going to live through the night! Just say the word Sol, I'll fucking kill him and make him disappear forever... " he shouted, fury and panic making him spit, his face is bright red.

"No Rigo, he's not worth it... where is Lily?" I plead.

"She came to get me! She shouldn't have to see this Sol, poor thing, she and Jason are with Nana but fucking hell Sol, you need to go to the hospital sis. He seriously messed you up!" The worry in his eyes jolts me back to my place in this hellish nightmare.

"You want some more bitch?! You're not a man you are a dog!" he screams as he lodges his foot into Brody's ribs.

I look at Brody, he must have taken a beating while I passed out, Rodrigo is sweating and he is bloody and curled up in a ball whimpering, flinching every time Rodrigo moves. I am so grateful for my brother from another mother at this moment tears come to my eyes that I can't hold back. Nine years ago we moved into this little two bedroom cottage in a predominantly Latino part of Los Angeles. We couldn't afford much more and seeing as my mixed heritage led people to assume I was Hispanic I had no worries about fitting in. In fact the neighbourhood felt like a family and everyone looked out for one another but expected the same in return. Gangs patrolled at night time but you knew it was as much for your safety as for their livelihood. No one came to our street who wasn't welcomed, the boys kept a good eye out and looked after the older residents. So long as the drugs and the violence was left to the gangs and on the streets no one said anything and just respected each person's place in the workings of this extended family. Rodrigo had been in the gang for the last eight years, we watched him step up to his responsibilities by choosing to leave school and do the only thing he thought he was good at, street life. He lived next door to us with Nana, who was his real grandmother but everyone called her Nana and his two younger sisters. Cousins and other grandchildren often stayed with Nana when things got bad in their own homes and she took in everyone, no matter what they had done. Her rules were simple, no drugs, no guns and a lot of respect. That was all that was allowed in her house, in return you would be showered with love, care and a hot meal at any time of day. I knew right now Nana had some cookies and milk dished out for the kids and was probably watching the Disney channel with them cuddled up on her super stuffed couch. She was the grandmother I never knew but always wanted and now I wished I had listened to her when she told me Brody would go bad all those years ago. Now the old woman was looking after his kids and I knew she was not going to let them go until he was gone... far away gone...

"Sol, I'm serious, I'm about to call an ambulance your head is covered in blood, there is blood on the doorframe and your clothes are ripped. What the hell did he hit you with?!"

"Jason's belt" I whispered.

"You serious! That's it this piece of shit is going tonight, no Cracker Jack junkie is going to do this and think I'm going to watch this happen."

Rodrigo rained down a few more punches on Brody, who by now was just a pathetic heap on the floor who kept whimpering. I knew on top of the beating he had taken that the pin pricks of his lack of brown were kicking in… he started gagging and shivering. I just hated him more but I knew I would never be able to live with myself if something happened to him at my own hands or hands that also pushed my kids on the swings in the park or cooked them snacks after school. Rodrigo was twenty-two years old, he was too emotional to deal with this in a way that would not change his life forever.

Me and Rigo were tight, despite the six years difference in age we were like twins. I knew him better than myself and often times we would meet up in the kid's treehouse, share a beer and dream. Dream about where we would go and what we would be. I would tell him all about my latest film projects and he would tell me about his adventures on the streets and all the girls that fell at his feet (or slapped his face). We shared everything, we were closer than any other siblings I had seen. Brody resented that so much but never made an issue out of it because he knew Rigo and his boys ran the streets here and as they were always ready to help me out around the house it gave him the chance to sneak off and work on his habit. The kids loved their Tio and whenever they saw him would follow him around or help him work on Nana's garden. He would take them out in his convertible and play his music loud and they thought they were the coolest kids alive. He attended to their sugar habit with great attention and frequent trips down to the market where, no matter how much I protested, he would take every chance he could to convince Nana that they needed fresh cookies and chocolate milk to share with him on the porch as the sun went down.

No. I could not let Rigo do anything to Brody, I knew he would kill him, I knew he could make people disappear but no, deep down he was good and deserved a life free from the same guilt I would feel if we got rid of Brody permanently. Besides, this crumpled up, shaking, pile of rotten flesh wasn't worth much more. He had killed any ounce of pity my love had turned towards, as much as I wanted him dead I still felt that pang inside me that knew somewhere deep within him was my love, my joy, my hero. Like a soldier he had been shot down and maimed, crippled by a barrage of pointed pricks that hunted out and killed his healthy veins and turned the light in his eyes into darkness. He had chosen that over us, he had chosen short term over long term and that never stopped hurting.

I stood up painfully again, turned to Brody now and felt like I was in complete control.

"Get up! You have twenty minutes to get whatever you want and then Rigo will take you down to the bus station," my voice sounding like an acidic witches curse.

"What you do from there is up to you but one thing you can not do is come anywhere near me and the kids. If I see you or any sign of you I will let Rigo unleash hell on you quite happily and I will dig the hole you will lie in. Do you understand?" I demanded.

"Soleil, please don't do this, help me clean up, remember you said you would. I can't do this on my own, I want to be with you forever, you are the only happiness I have in the world. Please Sol, give me another chance. I will leave and sort myself out; give me a few days then I'll come back and we can try again. I can't believe what I have done to you, I'm sorry please believe me I am sorry." He spilled out his pathetic begging like a scared little rat and tried to get up, apologise, beg and defend himself from Rodrigo all at once.

By this time he is on his knees and looking like a sinner repenting at the alter. His frame was racked with fear and uncertainty but sadly his mind was still only focusing on his fix. I know his going away for a few days is code for staying in a rat infested hole shooting up as much brown as he can score by stealing from me or any mug he can find. He'll come back then, sorry as anything and we'll carry on for a few months. I'll ignore his habit and watch him piss away all the money we pull in, money I wanted to have for the kids, money I wanted to take the kids to Mexico with and watch them run on those golden beaches and swim in that underwater paradise.

"Like I said, twenty minutes. I'm going to the bathroom to clean up as much as I can and you are packing you retched fuck. Take whatever you want, take the TV, the money jar, the bed I genuinely don't give a shit. Whatever you take is yours and that is the end of us. What you take is our settlement; you have no right to anything or anyone in these walls after the next twenty minutes. Rigo watch him but let him have whatever he wants and whatever his pathetic ass can carry. I don't want him coming back for anything so make sure he does a good job," I commanded.

"Brody, if you do not listen to what I am saying I am calling the police now. They will take one look at me and lock your pathetic ass up for a long time; then how will you fix up? You going to let those boys do you up the ass so you can pay for your supply. Tell him how it works Rigo, tell him what happens to a wife beating junkie when they go in..."

Rodrigo actually chuckles and his whole six foot six frame seems to relax as he imagines Brody in prison. "She's right prick, one phone call and the pigs will have you locked up. I'll tell them what I saw and make sure they know you had your hands around her neck and was not going to let her go. You were halfway to killing her when I got here and booted your ass off her. They'll believe me no doubt, the five-o around here know me and know how I look after my own. You will go down asshole and I'll chuckle the whole time.."

I searched out Brody's eyes one last time, a small part of me wanted to see that soul that once matched mine, the other part of my complicated heart that knew me and understood my unsettled being. I knew it wouldn't be there but I wanted to be sure. He had his head down; he knew the game was over. He was defeated and drawn out and the thought of the police was heavy in his mind.

"Look at me" I whispered.

He looked up quickly, hoping to be met with eyes of love and forgiveness instead meeting a searching cold stare. I searched, something inside me pleaded to find him but the pain and anger still racing around my body cut my compassion short.

"I thought so, you are dead inside, and I'll never forgive you for this Brody. Get up and twenty minutes start as soon as the bathroom door shuts. I'll leave your toothbrush outside on the floor."

I started walking towards the hallway, he got up and reached out to touch me as I passed, Rodrigo immediately jumped in front of him and punched his hand down.

"You will never touch her again, comprende?!"

"Goodbye Brody, take one last look at what you did to me, to us and to your kids. I loved you but now I don't, I just love the idea of being free from you and all the darkness you allowed to shadow the light we once enjoyed" I said calmly and softly.

His eyes welled up, but by now I could barely see him, one of my eyes was swollen shut and the other one had dried blood gluing my eyelids together.

“Soleiel, I’m sorry, please think about this” he pleaded.

“Twenty minutes, I’ll have a shower and clean up a bit then I want to come out to peace and quiet. I need to go see the kids are okay. You just go.” I reached out to find the wall and used it as a guide to get down the hallway and away from this unreal horror happening in my house.

I carried on walking, “Hermano, if he touches my equipment, murder him. Anything else let the rat steal away. He is going to need something to survive on and then he is on his own. My hands are clean.”

“Goodbye Brody” I called back over my shoulder as I limped down the hallway. “Please never get in touch or visit. By now I had reached the bathroom door, I walked in but didn’t turn on the light, I didn’t want to see what I had allowed Brody to do to me. I grabbed out at the toothbrush pot and chucked it outside. “Time starts now!” I shouted and slammed the door.

CHAPTER THREE

Now I had to turn the light on, I waited a few minutes and listened. I heard movement and Rodrigo cussing at him like a stinking dog that won't go outside. I knew he would be gone, I knew the future was what I had to look at now and the light switch was the first step.

My hand fumbled along the wall and found the switch. I flicked it and kept my eye shut as the bathroom brightness kicked in. I couldn't immediately look in the mirror and instead my eyes fell on the mosaic tile Jason had made at school last year, I could hardly make out the shape but I knew what it was by the raging red that jumped off the white wall. It was a heart that had the word LOVE in red tiles. I thought back to the day he brought it home. It was Valentine's Day and he was so excited to show me. I was working on my Mac when he came bursting through the door calling out to me and dropping his school bag all at once. I got up to go and meet him at the door but found Brody in the hallway, dishevelled and looking pist.

"Why did you wake me up you little shit?! Why are you always screaming in this house? I worked all night and this is the thanks I get!" He is snarling with as he looks down and his quivering little boy.

I quickly moved in front of Brody and scooped up Jason in my arms while we walked away and back outside. We sat on the porch and his little frame was almost totally enveloped in my lap. He was silent and his excitement seemed to have been extinguished.

Trying to change tactic and use distraction I cheerfully asked him, "What's got you so excited little man? Did you have a good day? How was your bus ride?"

He looked up at me with big crocodile tears in his eyes and stuck his bottom lip out.

"Don't cry baby, Daddy just had a long night at work, he doesn't mean it. What have you got there then?" He unfolded himself slightly but was still clutching a little package against his chest.

He looked hesitant but still excited and he took the package in both hands and told me "I made this at school, it is really just for you Ma. I don't want Daddy to have it or even see it. I made it just for you because it is Valentine's Day today."

I took the package he offered up and unwrapped the little LOVE tile. It was so beautiful and I knew he had worked hard to get it right. He never was good and the crafty stuff but this was so unique and so beautiful to me I welled up.

"Don't cry Ma, I made it because I love you!"

"I know baby, I just think it is the most wonderful thing I have ever seen and I want to keep it forever. Thank you."

Just then Brody walked out on the porch scratching his head and wincing at the sunlight. "Hey you two, how's it going? Whatcha got there Sol?" he asked me groggily.

"Just something Jason made at school, you ok?" I looked up at him, he had clearly just had a joint to take the edge off his need for a fix but as usual I ignored it and pretended all was well for the sake of the children.

"Ya babe, really good, hey little man that's great. Did you make that at school? We need to hang that up Sol."

So I did, in the bathroom, so every time I hid away in there to get some peace I could remind myself of the love I had, not the love I was losing.

With the light on and the clock ticking I knew I needed to turn around and look at what damage had been done. I could feel the sting on my back and I was sure two of my ribs were broken. Go to the hospital, ha, no way. All those people judging what my life had led me to and threatening to take my kids into care. Nah, I would call Chelsea in the morning and she would check me over. She may have left the neighborhood but she never forgot her friends. She was the pride of the street the day she graduated from med school. No one could believe that the pint sized brazen beauty who would turn her head to the books instead of boys had achieved her dream of being a doctor. She told us all the day she moved that she would only ever come back in a professional capacity and we all knew she had to leave and start fresh somewhere. Growing up here breeds a different sort of person and can crush your soul till you wake up one day and find yourself stumped by the reflection in the mirror. Ya, Chelsea would come back and check me over, she wouldn't judge, she never did. She knew the situation was never black and white. She used to clean up her mom after her dad would get a bit too friendly in a not so nice a way.

I gingerly turned around and looked at the mirror. I lost my breath and gasped. One of my eyes was swollen shut and the other one was caked in dry blood. My hair was a matted rat's nest and my forehead had blood crusted onto it. I had a welt across the left side of my neck and my shirt was ripped in six different places. I grabbed one of the holes and tugged. The material came away in my hands as I pulled the shirt down to my naval. Looking at the trail of marks, scratches and bruising I was disgusted, disgusted I didn't do anything to stop this and grateful it had been me not one of the children that had opened the door to him tonight. I am looking at this body, this lump of flesh that he tormented and took pleasure in destroying. And for what?! I looked at myself in disgust, already trying to figure out what to tell Lily when she sees me. She heard our argument for sure but at what point did she leave with Jason?

I decided that I will never let this happen again. I took out my phone, which was still in my jeans pocket and automatically started taking pictures. This was my back up plan, if he came back I would turn this over to the police and they can take over trying to manage that wretched thing that he has become. He always has gear of some kind on him so that will add to the charges and with California's three strike rule that would be his third damning strike and that's it; Done, peace at last and him destined to a lifetime of butt banditry and delusion. Why not do it anyway, why not call them now and have him put away? That was the nice part of me, the part that knew that at one point we were a unit, the other half of each other and the only person that mattered to each other. We were like a rainbow and never found the end, never hid from sight and were full of magic and light. We had nothing, but had it all, we stayed out all day and made the world our home. We were kids when we met, kids with broken homes but not broken spirits. We saw everything together and lived so many dreams I guess it was inevitable that it would turn into a nightmare at some point. But I had woken up from the nightmare now and I knew I was not alone; but not the other half of a soulful union either.

He always smoked pot, you grow up in Cali, you smoke pot, you enjoy life, you go watch the sunset and cook your dinner on the beach. We had no one at home cooking us a meal or waiting up for us, we just had life and the desire to live it to the ultimate. It's just part of who we are, what makes Cali the best place to be from, the best place to live and the place half the world want to get to! I guess for him the pot wasn't enough after a while, he wanted to journey, he got caught up with all the great rock bands who came out of here in the 80's and used to be a junior roadie for whoever was hiring. He would lie that he was eighteen and finished school, pack up a backpack and set of on these great adventures. I would tag along claiming to be an aspiring photographer and videographer. The bands ate it up and loved having young, dynamic people around them so we were an ideal pair. Les Affairs gave him his first hit of brown when he worked for their California Expulsion tour. He came back from that two week torrent of self-abuse and I was surprised how different he was. I had been with them the night he first tried it taking video footage of their show and pictures for my latest project. Brody on H was not a nice thing to see and the next day he swore to me he would never try it again because he said it felt like his bones were rattling and the back of his head had been blown out. He promised me, he told me it would just be weed and not even alcohol. I believed him and left the tour as I knew five days away from home was enough and someone would notice I was missing by now but when he came back I noticed he was quiet and sullen. The diamonds in his eyes had gone back to standard coal and he was tired. He told me he had tried it a few more times but that he didn't like it and he had left the tour early as he didn't trust himself to stay off it and knew if he came back to me he wouldn't need it. I doted on him, put my life to the side and just stayed with him every minute. I cuddled him and cooked for him and made sure he knew that we were the best thing that existed and we had no need for hard core shit like that in our lives. He never had any more for about 10 years and I thought the plague of H would never come back to fiddle with our perfection. In those ten years we set up in a mobile home by the beach, made movies, took pictures and lived like the most carefree children of the world. We grew up together and accepted the realities of the world. We understood that it was just us, no one would miss us or need us so we were free to grow, learn and love as we liked. Alas, another tour and an added 10 years of life and he felt he needed to turn back the clock, feel young and stupid again. This time it was the group Tourage Dam, a bunch of wannabe gangsters that sagged their trousers and rapped over their hard core rock. I was asked to cover their Santa Monica gig as they wanted a video montage of their

California tour so I took Brody with me as he was between jobs and he always got itchy when he had no money of his own. We watched the show and I personally thought their style was just fake, just about 'living the life' of a rock star but having no idea what integrity and self-respect were. Filming them back stage was almost sickening as they drank champagne from the bottle and fondled girls like they were petting cats. They played up for the camera and made life look good, time of their lives and stuff. Brody bought into that shit but I knew better, I'd seen it before, and I knew the band would be finished within a year. They asked Brody to come and smoke with them and then the drummer pulled out the brown and through pure peer pressure and lack of a backbone I watched Brody shoot up. I packed my camera and lights and left before he even took out the needle. When he came home two days later I was packed and ready to go. I handed him the keys to our little place near the beach and told him he could go fuck himself. He told me he was sorry and all the rest but that he had worked last night with the band on their Palm Springs gig and pulled out $500 cash. He said he did the brown just the once and the rest of the time he was just working with their head roadie trying to find an opening somewhere on the circuit so he could work again. I bought it and swallowed it just because deep down I didn't want to be alone. I didn't want to give up on my other half.

You can't explain what it feels like to realise you have been an idiot, you have deceived yourself and convinced yourself your life is as it should be. Looking in the mirror it seemed like every mark was screaming at me, condemning me and painting a picture of the hell I had been living for the last 5 years. The welts on my back represented the mountains I had constantly been battling whilst the bruises started to emerge like stains that could not be washed away. The blood painted a portrait of a silly girl, a stupid and scared child that held on to whatever happiness she could only to realise that no one actually cared about her and no one ever wanted to be her protector and guard. Looking at this tragic gallery I realised that from tonight onwards I would walk alone again, I would brace myself against the world, accept that soulfulness was genuinely adverse to joining me on my journey and accept that my happiness now lie in myself and the forging of an existence with my children. They had suffered enough and paid dearly for my self-deception and now it was going to be different. Instead of pacifying a beast I would cater to the blessings.

I ran the sink till it was warm and began to wash off the blood from my face. I wanted to see clearly and see what was left of me. I heard shouting outside the door and a new voice clearly shouting down the hallway. I knew Rodrigo would make sure what I said was done, he had wanted to kill Brody for the last five years and now he would be relishing the power he held and I felt safe now. He probably called a few of the boys in to make sure he left. The blood was easy to get off my head but to get it off my back was too painful for me. Every time I reached behind me my ribs screamed out for leniency and begged for attention. I gingerly got into the shower and let the hot water scorch me in a vain attempt to cleanse my body of its shame. I looked over at my jeans on the floor and my bloodstained rag of a shirt realising how lucky I was to be alive. I shut my eyes against the water and went back to the crystal waters of Mexico, I felt warmth and bliss and saw the colors of the sea once again, I smiled thinking of the calm I always know would wash over me when I go out to sea. The sea is where I always feel safe, I feel my inner restlessness disappear and I feel as though I will sprout gills at any moment and swim away like a fish cut from its hook; free to explore unknown places and never stop moving.

Looking down at the blood in the shower basin I realised that something else is bleeding and when I look at my back in the mirror I see six open welts seeping out blood like they are hiding a dirty secret. I groan and pray that it will soon stop as I can't bandage them and I needed to get over to Nana's to make sure the kids are ok. The bruises have come out to deepen my despair and I feel like my whole body will look like a pot of blue and black paint got thrown over me in the next hour. I turn off the shower and step out, I take one more long look at the wreckage the shower has salvaged, wrap a towel around it and sit on the toilet. I heard Rigo knocking softly on the door so I opened it a crack.

"Sol, babe you ok? Your face is a mess sis, damn. Please can I take you to hospital, you need to get looked at" he pleaded.

"Nah, I'm ok. I'll get Chelsea to come over tomorrow and clean me up some more" I barely whispered. "Is he gone Rigo? Will you keep him away?"

"Nah he is still rummaging around for something, says he can't find Jason's heart. What the fuck is he talking about? He is seriously messed up man."

I turn to the tile hanging on the wall and realise that manipulative asshole wants to get at me one more time. Probably to beg me to let him stay or slap me one last time, either way I'm not interested. As I turned around to take the tile off the wall Rodrigo gasps.

"What did he do to you? Why did you let him do this?! I told you he was shit, I told you to let me get rid of him! Why did you just take this?!" he shouts as he sees the damage written over my back.

"Rodrigo, not now, I know. You were always right. You and Nana have always told me and I never listened now I'm the painted fool. But just get him out of here please. Take him to the bus station he'll be high within an hour and that's it. He won't come back and if he does I won't open the door anymore, I'm done Rigo, look at this.."

I drop the back of my towel and show him the welts and bruises.

"I've learned my lesson now trust me, I'm done"

I passed him the heart tile, he could have it, I had Jason, I had love left. I hadn't injected it all away, I hadn't ignored what was real and I got to keep the prize.

"Give him this and go please, I want to get dressed and I want quiet. Please get him out of here."

"I can't guarantee you he'll get there alive sis, I can't let him get away with this..."

"Shut up and just do it my way, please, just get him gone and then get back here and go back to doing what you do best. Sit out on the porch smoke, drink do whatever just make sure he's gone."

I pleaded with him, "Don't walk away from this with blood on your hands especially that, its toxic and will come back to haunt you, just dump the trash and get back, life is going to continue without him tomorrow, I'll make sure of that."

Rodrigo, turned to go then took a step back and turned around, "Soleil, mi hermana, lo siento.." he tries to hug me but I know it will hurt so I stop him.

" I know bro, I know. It's not your fault its mine, it will all be ok. Just go. Please." I shut the bathroom door again and looked at the mirror again.

Life would be different now, it had to be, I had to be different. No point suffering this just to keep suffering. The replay button had been pressed and I was different, I could feel change in myself. Every injury was still pinching me and warning me to move on and away. Change your life Soleil, stop being changed and let your light shine.

CHAPTER FOUR

When silence was the only sound I could hear I cracked the door open and looked through the gap. Praying they were gone, I felt emboldened and threw the door open, dropped my towel and walked to my room completely nude. The air felt nice on my skin and I felt brazen, liberated and oddly in control. I walked into my bedroom and headed straight for my closet. I glanced at the bed but didn't linger. No need to share that with anyone anymore, I felt like if I climbed in I would sleep for days. I pulled out some long sleeved pyjamas and grimaced as they settled on my wounds and headed out the door again.

I walked very quietly, I wanted to hear the silence and enjoy the tranquillity as my mind was racing, screaming and totally confused. I thought I should be angry or sad but I was nothing, I was dull. I knew what happened had happened and I was safe from physical harm and so long as he stayed away from me no more mental trauma could be inflicted. I was calm, serene and not sad in the least. It was almost like what happened needed to happen and I knew this. It felt like the beating was my penance and that life would continue to something new now. I felt tranquil in the thought that this was me now, I was beaten, bruised, bloodied but not defeated. I felt lighter and flashes of optimism were popping into my head to interrupt the confusion. I could do what I wanted now, eat what I wanted and plan out each day exactly as I wanted. I would no longer spend hours trying to pacify the monster or hide his addiction. The children would have full run of the house now and I wouldn't shout at them if they screamed in the house or left their towel on the bathroom floor. No more shouting, no more anger, no more negativity. From today me and the kids would live life and enjoy as much of each day as we could in the sunlight not under a raincloud never sure when the thunder and lightning would start.

I got to the family room and the blood on the doorframe caught my eye but I walked further into the room. Rigo had done well, all of my equipment was still there and untouched. I still had my talents and I still had so many projects on that I could just bury myself here and find bliss. The money would come in, I never got much off Brody anyways and even if it didn't I knew we would be fine. My kids never demanded anything off me, they never cared about having the best things, it was all okay. I started to feel more confident that tonight was the beginning of a great part of my life, that I had rescued something and salvaged some integrity intact. I felt stronger and determined and so much lighter. I guess freedom always comes at a price but that duty had been paid now and life owed me back a bit now.

I started to notice little things were missing and things had just been pushed to the floor. He really did take all he could, if it had a value I didn't see it anymore. I was never attached to things, I never had much so I never understood how some 'thing' would ever control my actions or determine my mood. If I had a thing in my possession I would appreciate it and look after it but to cry if it broke or went missing; never. My mama would often beat be for that. She used to say "things come and go, hold onto the real treasures in life". I guess she was referring to herself and my lack of interaction with her but what a good lesson to learn young. Possessions never held a value or a meaning to me and I never felt tied to anything or required to spend spend spend. My attitude always made having no money easier to live with and made the world my treasure and wealth.

I walked around the family room, taking in the broken table the overturned chair and lamp. My throat ached and I never wanted to say another word. It was like I was silenced by the situation and silenced by a boulder in my throat that would turn to helpless sobs if I allowed it to. I got to the kitchen and stared at the unfinished potatoes I was working on when the bell went. I had diced the onions and had steak strips ready to grill. I had looked forward to our fajita night, the one night that always seemed to go well. We all sat down and everyone got to make their own version of glorious steak fajitas. Jason loved the guacamole while Lily devoured the sour cream. Brody smothered his meat in cheese and pickles and loved the super shredded Monterey Jack with jalapeños. I was just looking forward to sitting down and enjoying a moment of bliss, a little time free of demands and full of jovial conversations. Brody never messed those nights up. It was like he viewed it as a weekly penance for the blind eye treatment he enjoyed off me and he would make the most of it, laughing with the kids and telling them stories of his adventures on the road and the not so kind food he met on the way.

I decided to clear that up tomorrow, maybe I would do it for lunch, keep the kids home from school and celebrate with extra portions and no jalapeños. I'd get Nana to come and sit with us, a thank you for taking in the kids. I walked to the back door and put my slippers on. The back door was still open and I strode out onto the lawn and looked up even though the pain in my neck was burning. The stars welcomed me back to life, and greeted me back to the world I belonged in. Even through the pink haze of urban life, they twinkled and winked, reassuring me of safety and reaches I had yet to attain. I had a quick look around and opened the gate to the front yard. I walked out onto the lawn and nodded towards Carlos and Omar sitting in their BMW parked outside and felt grateful for their presence. I walked towards them as they hurried out of the car and raced towards me.

"Soleil, hermana, que te ha pasado?" Carlos asks worried.

"It got bad Carlos. Are they gone?"

"Rigo jumped in with his bat and that piece of shit and Marcos followed in his car. The punk took his car, so Rigo took the bat to it a bit just to send him off properly."

"Good, keep an eye out, I'm off to see Nana."

I walked up to Nana's house and started up the steps to the door. Carla and Yasmin were sitting outside under a blanket. They looked worried but still defiant; we shared a look of solidarity as I reached the top of the stairs. They knew what had happened, they saw this more then they needed to. This is what happened on the daily but they saw the look in my eyes. They knew that the boulder hadn't rolled down into a valley flooded by useless tears that only ravaged and didn't rebuild. Clara reached out her hand to me and held on.

"lo sieto Soleil, ti amo hermana" she whispered with care.

"Gracias chicas, te amo."

The screen door was unlocked and the door opened to the sounds of iCarly, one of Lily's favorites. I crept through to the family room and found the kids curled up either side of Nana. Lily, with her head on Nana's arm; clutching her arm to be sure she was not alone; and Jason curled up with his feet buried under the mountain of love which was his Nana, his own way of knowing safety was near. Nana had her glasses on and was praying. She looked up at me and let out a small whimper. I could see her heart breaking; she took in all the wounds and relived my pain. Sadness crept over her and she shrank a bit, suddenly her overstuffed sofa looked like it was engulfing her and the kids. She looked old and worn out, as if her marathon had no finish line and life was losing its lead on the pack.

“Hola Nana, pardon por ser un doler esta noche. Sorry to do this to you.” I choked on my words, the boulder teetering now, held in place by a matchstick.

“You don’t get to cry tonight my nina, tonight you be the rock and be strong. These two do not deserve this, my babies came to me shaking.” Her thick accent pronouncing every word carefully and with anger.

“I’ll make some leche and you will sit. These two angels will sleep here. They sleep while the night is ours to clear up. Come mija.” In spite of age, she maneuvered herself around her charges and untangled herself from them, placing the blanket over them all at once.

She reached out her hand as she passed me and gently placed it on my shoulder. She looked closely at the welt rising on my neck and winced. She said a prayer under her breath and carried on to the kitchen. After a few moments she covered up her sobs with the clang of pots and pans. I gave her a few minutes and then joined her in the kitchen. I sat down at my favorite spot and leaned back on the cushions. I sat up again quickly as pain was erupting on my back. Nana turned down the stove and came over, looking down the back of my shirt. She pulled at my shirt so I took it off but wrapped it protectively around my chest to save some modestly as my integrity was dwindling. She took in the bloodied battleground and walked off down the hall. She rummaged around the medicine cabinet and came back to the kitchen with supplies to try to ease my seeping soul.

She started working on my back and the sting of purification was relentless, she dabbed and tried to be as gentle as she could as she wiped away the seeping blood and soothe the welts. She turned away from my back to the stove and took the pan off the stove. She mixed in her mix of ground spice and magical fixers. She poured it out into my seaside mug and put it down in front of me.

"You not drinking Nana? Sit down and join me."

"Give me a minute, I think you might need that second cup more than me." She set off trying to bandage by back with whatever she had available. Unfortunately, no band-aid was big enough to erase the past.

"That's enough Nana, thank you. Sit down please." as I pulled my shirt back over my head.

We sat in silence, we had no words to share. Silence was the only sound that could keep the balance of this moment as it was and serenade calm to come back over us. I finished my leche and Nana refilled my cup. The clocked ticked on and we sat. She started her quiet prayers again and I was grateful, I may not believe like she did but I was grateful God had kept me here. I had been saved tonight. I had suffered but was not broken and the burden I shouldered was lighter, fading with the stars and the white line of the new day that was breaking.

Rodrigo came in and interrupted the silence. He took in the scene, looked at Nana and smiled. "Any leche left for me Nana?"

"Of course Nino, and the kids left you some cookies in the family room."

"He's gone Sol, we took him and left him there then followed his sick ass till he crawled in a hole.

The boys will keep an eye out don't worry, that punk bitch will never be allowed on this street again."

"Cuida tu lenguaje! Don't swear here!" Nana scolded.

"Lo siento Nana." He replied.

"Thanks bro, enjoy the cookies." This prompted him to grab his drink and walk off. I watched him wiggle his way between the kids and readjust the blanket. With his plate of cookies he smiled and was a kid himself watching Carly and her brother throw a surprise party for Sam. I smiled, that idiot loved Disney channel, and he never minded watching whatever was on. He got defensive when you asked him what his favorite show was, but it was just a joke. Watching idealistic white Americans 'making it' and having fun and every day having a happy ending was far away from his reality. Why not enjoy a bit of fantasy, it was better than porn.

Eventually the dawn chorus sang forth its capturing of the rising sun. My eyes felt heavy and I just wanted to sleep. Nana ushered me into the guest room that was always ready. Fluffy pillows and warm clean comforters awaited whatever pain and distress you could throw at them.

I slinked in under the covers and she kissed my head. "Don't worry mija, the kids won't leave my sight and I'll tell school they are not coming today. You rest" she cooed as I raced off to exhaustion and met sleep halfway.

CHAPTER FIVE

I stayed huddled under the comforter and hung on the scraps of sleep that alternatively soothed me then tormented me as soreness set in. No dreams just rest, no thoughts just exhausted healing. I heard the door creak a few times and I knew the sun was bright in the sky but I struggled to open my eyes and take in the new day. I remembered one was swollen so I worked on getting the other one to work again. I took in the room and lie in bed looking up at the lampshade. The impending life that awaited the first step I took out of this bed made me hesitant and I turned back over and reburied myself under the blankets.

Eventually, Jason could no longer be contained and I am sure he had creaked the door open at least four times before he could no longer venture in on silent missions. He determidly pulled back the blankets this time and the bed jiggled as he climbed in and buried his head into chest and said "Ma, it's 1230, can you get up now so I can see you please?"

My body was so sore and crippled by pain. The raw injuries I had suffered had barely relented in their torture and his head felt like a hot iron burning into my skin. I bit my lip and tried to smile through the pain but winced and groaned.

"See me, I was here all the time baby." I said softly, breathing out slowly to stop myself from throwing up.

"Ma, your eye is black and you have cuts on your face and head. Are you okay?" he asked almost sheepishly.

"I'm hurting Jason but I won't be soon. I'll be as good as new before you know it. But Daddy is gone baby, he said he had to go away for a while..."

"Good!" he interrupted. "Can you tell him not to come back? I don't like him anymore" he asserted.

"I'll see what I can do baby. I don't really want to see him for a while either."

We had a painful cuddle and I gave him a kiss on his sandy locks.

"Have you had your breakfast yet? Did Nana make pancakes?" I asked trying to sound like I normally did.

"She sure did Ma! She put chocolate chips in mine! She never does that but she said today was special and I was special so I deserved a treat! Lily didn't eat much, she is sitting on the couch and won't move, she says she is waiting for you to get up."

"Did she sleep on the couch?" I asked racked with an overwhelming guilt.

"Ya, she did. Tio picked me up at some point cause I woke up in his room. He got chocolate chip pancakes too!" he told me excitedly.

My stomach sank, Lily was going to be a mess; she would be so confused.

"Jay can you go tell Lily to come see me please. Then I want you to have a shower stinky boy! Tell Tio to go get you some clothes from home!" I tried to sound happy and jokingly tussled his hair and gave him a little squeeze.

"Ok, but I think we are going to fly his helicopter first Ma, is that okay? He is out front and said I could hold the remote!" He said as he scampered out of the bed and towards the door.

"Liiilly!" He shouted from the door. "Ma wants you!"

She must have been waiting on tenderhooks to hear that. I immediately heard her angel-light footsteps running towards me. She got to the door before Jason had even left the room and was panting. My gorgeous little girl looked tired, strained and stressed. Her wavy golden brown curls were sticking out in all directions and frizzy. Her angelic blue eyes were clouded over with a mixture of fear and lack of sleep. She was still in the clothes she put on after she came home from school yesterday and after seeing my face she looked horrified.

"I'm going to fly the helicopter Lily! Ma said I could!" Jason squealed as he ran past her down the hallway.

I looked at my little treasure and didn't trust myself to speak so instead I opened up the comforter and scooted over so she could climb in bed with me. She hesitated and almost recoiled when she saw a hint of what injuries my pyjamas covered, but her love took hold and she came and crawled in next to me.

"Ma, can I cuddle you or does it hurt too much?" she whispered.

"Let me cuddle you baby, don't be sad. I'm okay, I'll be back to normal as quick as I can."

"But your eye Ma, and the cuts. Why did he do this to you? I hate him!" she blurted before she burst into tears. The sobs that came forth from her shook her little lithe frame. She couldn't control them and the whole bed shook as her waves of sadness spilled over us. I couldn't think of one word to say. She knew what had happened and she knew how much I was hurting but trying to hide it. My poor girl was a wreck. I held her as tight as I could, I wanted to hold her and take all of her hurt, sorrow and anger away. She deserved a better life; she shouldn't have to be a part of abuse of any kind. She has the kindest soul that ever was created and I knew she was shredded inside. I could almost feel the hollowness and the screams echoing inside her and shook her whole body.

"You cry Lily, get it all out. Don't stop. I promise this is the last time you will cry for me baby. I made him go this time. You and I will look after Jason now and no more of this."

She slowly stopped sobbing and her body jolted with hiccups. "Really Mama, he's gone?"

"He is gone. He took some of our special things but I don't mind so much do you?" I asked.

She looked at me in disbelief. "Gone? You sure?"

"Yes my love. Will you miss him?" I asked realising that I was effectively telling my daughter she was not going to see her dad again!

"I might miss him Ma, he used to be nice sometimes and he let me help him build things. Sometimes he would tickle me until I couldn't breathe and his pancakes were always so yummy. Will you be mad if I miss him Mama?" she asked suddenly looking worried.

"Of course not, and you can talk about him too I don't mind. I knew him a long time and he was my best friend. If he really wants to he will come visit I am sure and if he doesn't then we will remember happy things and try to make our pancakes even better!" I joked as I went in to tickle her, my ribs twitching and reminding me of their distress.

She giggled and smiled closing her eyes so as to not see my pain and grimace; I knew this new life would be lonely but my little girl would be the lamp to guide us and I would do whatever and say whatever to make sure she was happy.

"I'm going to call Chelsea baby, can you give me a minute? Jason said there are chocolate chip pancakes in the kitchen. Go and have a few and I'll come join you in a few minutes." I kissed her head and gave her a squeeze.

"Ok Ma, but can you get up? I can bring you some pancakes if you want."

"Ok, but only if you join me for breakfast in bed."

She flashed me a glowing moonbeam smile and ran out of the room. I picked up my phone, dreading the idea of any communication from Brody. No messages, no missed calls, nothing... perfect. I knew he was high as a kite somewhere and I was probably the last thing on his mind. This thought made me happy and refreshed the sense of freedom I had felt the night before. I looked up Chelsea and made the call, I knew she had most likely heard from Rigo so it was no surprise when she picked up straight away.

"Hey Chelsea, how are you?"

"Hell of a lot better then you are Sol. What kind of mess do you need me to clean up now?!" she asked, angry and frustrated.

"What can I say? If I told you I got rid of him and it's never going to happen again would you believe me?"

"No, never. My momma said the same shit for 15 years!"

"Well if I told you that Rodrigo got him out and I've told Lily her daddy is gone would you believe me then?"

"You told Lily what?"

"What else could I say, she saw the beating, she ran to Nana's house to get Rigo and she saw the state I was in this morning. What should I tell her?! Don't worry baby, daddy will be back. Your mom is an idiot and I enjoy having the shit kicked out of me so can't wait for him to come back!" I started coughing as my throat was still sore from being choked out.

Chelsea stayed quiet, I knew she was upset and worried about Lily. "He's gone Chel, I never want anything to do with him. I want some of my life back. I need to protect the kids. Today it is me tomorrow it will be one of them. You know this is true. He's gone. Gone from the house and our lives."

"I gave Rigo permission to kill him if he comes back." I finished with, slightly smiling.

Chelsea chuckled on the other end, "Now I know you are serious. I'm here for you Sol, all three of you. Give me an hour, I'll swing by CVS and get some stuff to clean you up. Do you need painkillers?"

"No way, none of that shit. I'm good. Bastard hit me with a belt, I feel like my back is burned and I'm just so sore, especially my throat."

“Well what do you expect, according to Rigo you are lucky he came in when he did. He said you were passed out and the asshole was still choking you!”

“Ya.” I sighed. “I guess it was really bad. I’ll see you in a bit.”

“Love you Soleil, it will be ok, promise.”

“Ya, I know babe. Thanks, I’ll see you soon.” I hung up. Suddenly hit by the enormity of what happened. I was two minutes away from death. My kids could have been orphans today; but I survived and I was here. Life was mine now for the taking.

“Mama! You won’t believe how many pancakes Nana made! She is bringing one thousand and she is going to eat breakfast in bed with us too!” Lily interrupted my thoughts with her excited announcement.

“Move over Mija. Me and my pancakes are joining you. You need to eat so you can go out front and tell off Rodrigo. He has your son flying planes driving the dog crazy!” She said with just the right mix of love and fierceness. I knew Nana was not going to let me out of her sight. She sat next to me and dished out three pancakes for Lily and started cutting up mine.

“Nana.. I can..”

“Shush Mija, just shush and let someone look after you” As she started feeding me not just her pancakes but much needed forkfuls of love.

CHAPTER SIX

Time, life, love and fate. They all move so quickly and stir such odd reactions. Sometimes you just do crazy things and only realize later that you only got halfway through your reasoning before you acted. Pain, despair and disappointment disturb your thoughts and hurt your heart. People you love and trust become enemies and cause you to remember that you were never anything special to anyone ever. The shame in that is it took you so long to realise it and that you never even contemplated to tell the world to jump off a bridge and to focus on loving yourself. Then you are further depressed by the fact that time and love are man-made creations that distract you; whilst life and fate are gifts you take for granted and neglect at your peril.

I always lived in the present, working on the moment I was in, capturing what I could of the here and now. My past was too painful and a future was not a guarantee so I just assumed it wasn't there yet. Kindness was what I worked with and when this was met with hurt, hate and pain I would stumble back and hide in fear and shock at the lack of humanity and care that was out there. I was never bold, never brazen, never the one to stand up for myself or make a situation revolve around me. Instead I hid behind a camera and accepted that the world was cold, cruel and it was best to sit out, not join in as I didn't understand the rules and was most likely going to fail miserably. I lived in my own world, trusted no one, spoke to no one and looked after myself. The world of womanhood seemed a series of scientific experiments I had no idea how to run. Beauty and fashion seemed a waste of time as I had more important things to focus on, namely survival. The few attempts I made failed, garnished me unwanted attention and ultimately led to more assumptions and pain. I stayed plain, I focused on true happiness, I focused on what was real and what I was; not on what was fake and incomprehensible. Growing up you have very little power over your life and what happens to you. My dad was never around as he worked as a long-haul driver and by the time I was walking had fallen out of love with Momma. They tolerated one another and fought at every chance they got. They would fight and scream but the next day their door was locked and fury turned to passion. This left me and my sister to our own devices.

By four I knew how to make my own breakfast, by eight I could drive a car. My introduction to womanhood was "You're a woman now, go get some pads and shave your pits." and my night time routine included tucking in Momma with either Jack or Bailey so she could see them first thing in the morning and reassure herself that alcohol still loved her and probably would love her to death. I started leaving home at eleven and escaped by being useful to people I knew or finding sympathetic parents in my friend's houses who would let me stay a few nights. I could be the highest, drunkest kid at the party and I didn't have to worry because even if I did go home there was no one there to tell me off or even notice how young and fucked up I was. The one therapist I saw once told me that physical and sexual abuse are horrible, but he said the worst abuse he had ever seen is emotional abuse and neglect. He told me that I would have to be so strong because I was a victim of three of those abuses but I could conquer them. I felt invigorated as someone had finally understood. I had a badge I could wear and a prescription people could understand and thus help me. As soon as the school made budget cuts he was gone and this left an enormous seeping wound inside me. I felt the last ship had sailed and help was now dried up. No one would understand me now, no one would want to come anywhere near me and my problems. I was alone. Then I started high school and Brody came into my life and he possessed me almost immediately. He protected me and loved me, pushed me to make films and photographs, took me all over LA and waited patiently for me to trust him, hear him and ultimately love him back. Too bad once you are a victim you always seem to remain one. I was a victim and the support and sympathy never emerged, apologies never came forth and healed me. Today I was victim number one, but the self-pity I felt had gone and just like everything else I would bare my burden quietly, trust no one, rely on no one and definitely not give my heart away. I would focus on Life and try as hard as I could to find a fate that didn't require constant payment in pain and emotional hurt.

The week that had passed had really crawled past. The kids had a day off school and Nana helped me but the house back together. Chelsea came and repaired what she could and bandaged me up. She cleaned up my back but I could feel her hand shaking the whole time.

We all slept in Lily's bed, holding on to each other and knowing the boys outside would keep any intrusion away. We laughed and smiled, hugged a lot and told each other we loved each other too much. I felt numb and on autopilot most of the time. The pain and soreness of my body was too much to handle at times and always a reminder of what I had gained and lost. We had one more week of school till summer break and I had no idea how we were going to pass away the next three months but I needed to get a massive project done, this much I knew.

Life flowered, life pulled us along and healed the wounds that fate had left behind. I hadn't been able to get back to work on my latest project but I knew inspiration would come and with all the back footage I had, creating a biopic on Zephyr would be one of my more enjoyable projects. Their record label always had projects for me and one day when they asked me who my favourite band was Zephyr won hands down.

They were a punk pop phenomenon and the best live performers I had ever seen. Their music always touched me and spoke to me like a mystic, like a lost friend and poet. They were a very handsome foursome and chivalrous and kind to those who waited hours to meet them. They came from LA and loved LA which always makes music sound richer to me. They had survived through the death of their drummer, drug addiction, a plane crash and changing tastes in music to still pack out a stadium any day of the week. Filming them was easy; they played to the camera and always had fun but kept their individuality, integrity and intelligence on display. True masters of the English language I always admired how they spoke so confidently and always looked to play on the words of the journalists that tried to goad them into salacious soundbites or awkward conversations.

The kids and I always played their albums and Lily came with me to their last concert at the Rose Bowl. Her dad had disappeared again so I took her with me instead. She thought I was the coolest mom ever and she was definitely the coolest kid in her class once word had got out.

In almost every other way it was surprising how easy life picked up again in a week and how easy it had been to adapt to not having Brody around. I had had no phone calls or messages and to be honest that was better. I found myself with free time not taken up by his anger and self-destruction cycles. The kids and I took bike rides to go have dinner, we played cards at Nana's house and even had a picnic in the treehouse. I started to relax as I healed and with every bruise and cut that mended a small part of my soul was restored. The boulder in my throat never dislodged but took its time to downgrade to a pebble. I knew if I ever started crying I would take a long time to stop. So I made Brody into a movie of his own, a cinematic experience I was part of in 4D. I remembered all of the good times, the secrets we shared and the love and passion I knew I would never relive. I wanted Brody to be something I had loved and lost not something I hated and wanted to destroy.

Rodrigo practically moved in which was a great comfort. He used the excuse that one of Nana's nieces had lost her job so she had come to visit Nana with no fixed date on when she planned to leave. Once the kids went to sleep we would sit out on the porch and carry on with our dreams and think out loud for each other's benefit.

"So what now sis? You gunna stay here or move on somewhere nice and closer to the sea?" he asked me about ten days after Brody left.

"Why would I do that Rigo? Don't be silly, he won't come back and if he does I told you, you have my permission to kill him." I said this with a mocking smile as his gangsta attitude was often a source of my laughter.

"I swear if I see him I will fuck him up" he said fiercely.

"Ya ya, I am sure you will. Make sure you tell Carlos I appreciate him staying nearby at night time. The other night Jay woke up scared and I showed him Carlos parked outside and he told me it felt like he had angels keeping watch."

"Carlos ain't no angel Sol!"

"I know but the reality the kids know and understand wouldn't make sense to most people but for us it works and yes, people like you and Carlos, as messed up as you are and as violent as I know you can be will always be their angels. They trust you and know you would never hurt them."

"Nah, I would never hurt those two, they are like my own flesh and blood" he mumbled as he tried to casually rub his eyes.

"You are a big softie you know. One day when you have your own kids you are going to be a pushover" I joked.

"Shut up, I am hard as a rock, no way my kids will be spoiled" he said trying to be tough.

"Ya sure you are" I smiled.

"Hey you know that thing you are doing on Zephyr? I got some news for you now sis!" he said desperate to change the subject.

"Really? What's that then?"

"You know Carlos has a brother, Gordo?" he asked

"Of course I know Gordo"

"Well you know he's a dealer right, so apparently he delivers an pound of weed to Zephyr's lead singer at least every two months." he told me smugly.

"Wow Rigo, best news I've heard. Why would I want to know this?"

"Maybe he can take you to his house and you can sit down properly and interview him or something for this movie. I dunno, I just thought it might be useful for you."

"Useful to know he smokes a pound of weed every two months and has it delivered by a fat man with terrible taste in clothes? Perfect, I will somehow get that into the film and then go and work for the National Enquirer to ruin every stars chance at privacy!"

"Huh?" he asked genuinely dumbfounded by my reaction as he knew I loved the group and would have jumped at any chance to be in the same zip code as them before.

"No way would I ever leak that little titbit out on film. The dude probably has back pain or something and smokes a little to relax. No harm in that, come on, you go through a pound in about a week right?!" I laid down accusingly.

Rodrigo went serious on me and sat up straight, he looked at me sternly and said "Since that night Sol I don't want to touch anything. I have been clean and sober. I can't sleep much and I've had a beer here and there but otherwise I don't want to touch anything. After seeing that hole your ex-rat climbed down and the people that were there and the damage he did to you how can I go get high and think there will be no consequence?"

He shuffled his big size 13 feet and looked down at the wood planks of the porch. I knew he wanted to tell me something serious but probably thought I would laugh at him.

"Nah, I think I am going to take a little break from killing myself and start thinking about a serious future. DO something positive with my life. I'll always stay true to the barrio and I know I have to look out for people but I don't want to die without having done something good with my life. Nana told me I should try getting into cooking. She taught me ever since I was a kid and I love it."

"That's true, you are one of the best chef's I know! Don't tell Nana but your cookies are better than hers!" I interrupted.

"Ya, I add a few things she doesn't know about. So seriously I am thinking of trying to get some work in a fancy place and maybe one day have my own restaurant." He said with a twinge of nervousness.

"Rigo that would be amazing! You can totally do that! Get into a really good place and just make a rep for yourself. You can save up and have your own place in no time! We would all support you bro, you know that and the barrio would be your best clients!" I was genuinely excited by the prospect of him dressed in a white jacket cooking up a storm! He was always trying out new things and getting the kids to try out his new recipes. He definitely had the talents and definitely had the determination and love required.

"Ya, I'm serious sis, Gordo said he would fund me too. Thing is I think I need to go into a kitchen and test the skills out on a real life restaurant. See what it's like to feed people in that kind of setting.

Making sure I get it all right, learn the tricks and maybe pick up some new ideas" he said with a wistful look out onto the front lawn.

"Why wait for someone to teach you what you already know! Get your own little van and start travelling around selling your dishes. Rigo, move on this, don't sit still or let the rejection of so called 'gourmet chefs' tag you with a label. If Gordo has the funds get a van, fix it up and go out there to the people and cheer them up with some good food. If you hit the swap meet on Sunday with your fajita surprise and macaroni mayhem you would sell out in an hour!"

"You really think so?"

"Absolutely! Nana would help you get started to and I'll be there getting people to try it. Trust me Rigo, start off on your own and let the professionals either watch you with envy or beg you to come join them."

"You are right sis, my own van.. I can go where I want, open when I want and change up the menu when I want. Total control and no big boss breathing down my neck!"

"Seriously, that is the best thing I've heard you say bro. You would be the man and the people would be lining up for your grub! And the ladies

Rigo! Watch out, they will be all over you... fine young man, owns his own business, cooks like a pro...." I started giggling.

"Ya, totally see that sis...it would be amazing..." he said dreamily.

I stared out in silence and we both sat there contented with the genuine prospect of a new life for him. My mind drifted off and I was happy that something good had come out of the horrors of ten days ago. It would be so nice to see Rodrigo succeed at this and create a positive life for himself. Having dreams was crucial to life. Dreams are what keep you focused and alive. Dreams give you a reason to wake up in the morning and work hard instead of falling into a dull drum existence. Dreams were the best part of my life, dreams took me on so many adventures and gave me so much pleasure. Brody and I lived for dreams and loved our life together. My wistfulness started to die off when I realised that I was out of dreams. I had been so focused on surviving, modifying and adjusting to life with and without Brody that I hadn't once thought about what I was going to do now. I trudged along with my movie work but maybe this was the time to explore even more, create new dreams, set new targets for myself. Maybe move by the sea, teach the kids how to surf and have bonfires and barbeques on the beach. I became aware that time was passing and Brody was gone gone, life was still ticking by and I was still young and able. I realised I lost track of that bold resolve that had come over me, that I would love, protect and enjoy being a mother and take more care in the children and creating a better more stable life for us. Instantly my mind started making a checklist of tasks to get through. Number one on the list was dream new dreams, number two – start looking for a place by the sea.

CHAPTER SEVEN

I settled back into the usual summer routine quite quickly and another two weeks passed. I would work on my mini movie in the morning then spend the rest of the day with the kids. Living in the barrio was excellent at times, we had people we could trust and they genuinely looked after each other. We suffered the violence, drugs horrors and domestic unrest, but we suffered together and supported one another. My kids were your kids and your kids were mine. If Lily walked in with Miklo from across the road and three of the neighbors and it was dinner time well you shared out and fed everyone. That was the way it was, that was the family we knew and loved.

The next day after lunch, we headed straight to the beach for Rodrigo's birthday bash. He was so excited. He was hosting a beach barbeque to try out his recipes and get people interested in his new food ideas.

He had found a beat up taco wagon and was having his boys work on it to bring some life back to it and add his own personal touches. But today was just an old school drum barbeque, classic recipes and plenty of music, drinks and sunshine.

Nana's girls had set up her Christmas lights on poles and had flags and sheets hung up that were blowing like rainbows in the sky. When the sun went down Rigo stoked up a bonfire and dessert was s'mores and caramel popcorn. We all had a dance and then sat around the fire just enjoying the simple pleasures we had been blessed with. The kids performed a song for their tio and then pulled out a badly wrapped box from the car. They brought it over and set it down in front of Rigo full of pride.

"What's this my little locas?"

Timidly and shuffling her feet Lily took out a piece of paper from her pocket. Jason was staring at her with big eyes and absolute admiration for her bravery. She started really quiet but got confident as she read her poem.

"Tio can do anything, he even flies at night

He makes us cookies and helps if people have a fight

He is the best to watch iCarly because he laughs really loud

He wants to make a restaurant now and make Nana proud

We love his food and know he will do well

Our Tio is the best, he is an an-gel."

I was stunned into silence, I was touched by how simple she had summed up Rodrigo and understood how important he was to her. Jason cut in.

"I came up with the last line! But Lily did the rest! Open the present Tio!"

He came out of his surprise at the poem and looked at the present.

Rodrigo ripped open the paper, the kid in him bursting back to life. He got to the box and gasped, "No way..."

"No way a KitchenAid all in one! How did you...?" Rigo was genuinely surprised and so was I! I had no idea they had done this or where they had even bought the present from. Then I looked at Nana and she winked. I slipped next to her on the bench and gave her a kiss.

"Thanks Nana, the kids must feel like they are ten feet tall. When did you do this?"

"Carla helped me." she smiled.

"Ma did you like our surprise! You didn't even know about it!" Lily came bouncing over so excited her plan had worked. Jason trailed behind like a little assistant.

"It was amazing Lily, you and Jason are so smart! I think you got Tio and Nana a perfect present!"

Jason climbed up into Nana's lap for a cuddle, he was tired and done with all the excitement of the day. Lily sat on my lap and leaned her little frame up against my chest. She smelled like the sea and sugar. I sat there holding her and looking at Jason, this moment was perfect. I wanted to hold on to it, frame it and keep living it. The night was perfect, our bellies were full, Rigo was already reeling off the thousands of things he could do with the KitchenAid to his friends; I had to laugh, looking at the boys surrounding a kitchen tool and discussing guacamole and salsa mixes was a far cry from their usual chat about their daily business.

"Whats so funny Ma?" Lily whispered.

"I'm just really happy Lily. Tonight was perfect and everything is amazing. You and Jason made this night even more perfect" I said as I gave her a big kiss and held her even tighter.

Waves and waves of happiness found their way back into our life. Jason and I were working at our vegetable patch on the side of the house when we heard an unhappy voice calling from the front.

"Hola, Brody! Are you home?"

"Just a minute" I called trying hard to place the voice with the person before I came face to face with them. I came to the front of the house only to find our Landlord Xavier standing there. Just seeing him filled me with dread. He would only be here if there was a problem. He owned five houses in this area and lived really nicely off the rent he collected in San Bernardino. For him to come down here, must be something serious.

"Hi Xav, how are you? I wasn't expecting a visit from you" I said as cheerfully as possible.

"Soleil, we need to talk. We have a small problem."

We went inside the house and I sent the kids outside to continue work on the garden as I had a bad feeling this conversation was no going to be a joyful one.

"I cut to the point Soleil, you owe me $4,600 in rent and I need you to either pay that to me by next week or move out. I have had nothing from you in four months now, I spoke to Brody two months ago and he said he put a check in the mail to cover six months. I got the check but it bounced so I spoke to him again and he said he would do it by western union. Still nothing and now he doesn't answer his phone so I have to bring this to you I'm afraid."

"We are four months behind on rent Xav? How in the world did he manage to do that?! I gave him six months of rent money four months ago and he walked into the bank, told me he deposited it and that we were going to be okay for six months. You know how we always did Xav."

"Soleil you guys have been the best tenants for ten years, I would never say this if it wasn't true. But I have had nothing in four months and now I am feeling the debt and I need it to be paid or else you have to move out. I'm sorry but I have a family to support too" he said with an apologetic hint in his voice.

"No, Xav. I get it. I am just so shocked that he did that. He must have spent that money or did something. It never came back here and if it didn't go to you then..." I held my face in my hands. I had been a stupid and trusting fool. I should have never left him in control of the rent and house payments! I thought rent would be something I would worry about in two months which would be after I got paid for my Zephyr project.

"So what options do I have now? You know Brody is gone and never coming back. That punk took my money and now he's gone Xav it is just me and the kids here now." I was trying not to sound angry but failing miserably.

"Look, it is no my fault girl. You know I leave you alone, fix the problems and just ask for rent to be on time. I have an eviction letter here I have no choice but to give you. I put the date for repayment at two weeks from now and if you pay you stay but then remember that rent for this month is also due in two weeks so you need $5,800 and we are good. If you can't pay I am sorry but you will have to move out."

"We have nowhere to go! Where am I going to go with the kids! I have no relatives around here and all our stuff..." I sniffled and realised I was incredibly angry at this point. As if we hadn't been through enough!

I got myself together and looked at Xavier. He was looking at me with concern. I knew he didn't like to be the bad guy and he had had it rough growing up. But him and I knew business was business and you pay what you owe or move on.

“Sorry, it’s not your fault. I will take the letter just because I have to and appreciate the two weeks to get things sorted. I will try to get your money together but I don’t think it will happen if I am honest. I get small royalties for my work and pictures but truth is if I give it all to you I have nothing to feed the kids with. We will be out in two weeks, I promise and we’ll leave the place nice and neat for you. I will try to pay you back the $4,600 as soon as possible, I won’t run off for good I promise. You have been good to us and I will do whatever I can to pay you back all of the money just be patient please.” I sounded completely defeated; I couldn’t even look up at him.

“Soleil, you are a strong and brave woman. I know you will pay me back and I know you will do what you say. You take your time and make sure you find somewhere for you and the kids first. I can wait. Anyways, I am going to charge the next people who come in here more so I’ll make my money back don’t worry.” He got up to leave gently placing the envelope with the letter on the table between us.

I composed myself and stood up slowly. We walked towards the front door and I opened the screen to let him out.

"Take care Mija, I really wish I could help but.." he was now close enough to see the remaining bruising and welt on my neck, his words got stuck.

"I know, I know.. I appreciate your help already. Let me walk you out." "Thanks Xav, this place has been amazing for ten years and I really appreciate all your help in the past. I'll leave you my contact details so we can work out repayment. Take care of yourself"

"Adios Soleil. Take care of yourself" he responded kindly as he made his way off the porch towards his flashy BMW.

"All I have ever done is take care of myself" I thought. What's new now? Two weeks to find a new place to live. Two weeks to pack up our whole life and take it somewhere new. The kids would be horrified to leave Nana and Rodrigo but they had no room for us. Anyways I wouldn't ever ask as I know the people Nana let live with her needed her more than we did now that Brody was gone.

Well you wanted to find a place by the sea, here is your chance! I knew I had to take this as fate and karma kicking me forward and deeper into a new life. I knew this was the motivation I needed to start something new and get my life back. But with no money what would I do. I had about $1000 saved up for an emergency but that was it. I had the Zephyr project to finish and that would be a big payday but I still had a month to go on that so what do we do in the meantime?!

I walked out onto the porch and watched Xavier drive off. I sat on my favorite step and just let memories wash over me for a few minutes. Each one came in quick and filled with light but too many left with a dark cloud over them or sadness sounding off in the background. I knew we had to go to be completely free of the past, but it wouldn't be easy leaving the love and trust we had here. Finding a surrogate family had been a blessing and had ultimately saved my life, and now I had to leave it. Dread filled my chest and rooted itself firmly. All that I cherished would have to be let go now and I would have to seriously think about what next? Even though he was nowhere to be seen Brody had abused us one last time. He had let us down and was relentless and ruthless in his torment.

I stood up and squared my shoulders, put my head up high and remembered the new determination I had found that fateful night. I would tell the kids tomorrow; today we would enjoy our garden and enjoy no stress, no worries.

I would save all that for me alone, I would only think about the reality we now had to face tonight once they were asleep and peaceful.

Later that night I told Rodrigo what had happened. He was shocked and angry as usual but then he just got quiet.

"Don't worry sis, next week I'll have $5,800 for you cash. You take that to Xavier monster mogul and shut him up."

"Hey! Don't be like that, it is not his problem. He owns a house and needs the rent to survive. Where is the crime in any of that?"

"I know, but you have been here a long time and you always paid on time, looked after the place and made this place a home." His voice crackled a bit and I knew he was choking up on me again.

"Hey, punk! Listen I may need to move but I'm not dead! This might be an answer to my prayers Rigo. I need a fresh start, kids need space and I want to see the sea in the morning when I wake up. You know Palisades or Malibu..."

"Don't forget where you are coming from gringa! What's wrong with the hood?! At least you got love here!" he said with hurt in his voice.

"Bro you know Nana would be the first one to tell either of us to get the hell out. She hates this place and now she's old and just wants to relax. Besides, you want me to do better than I am right now don't you? What about the kids? They could go to a better school and learn to surf..." I trailed off as there was no need to explain further. We had had this conversation one hundred times and he always knew I was right and one day we would move and not be so close anymore.

Our usual silence filled the treehouse. We knew it was late, we knew we wouldn't be neighbors forever and we both knew this was a blessing in disguise.

"Hey, speaking of Malibu I went to Marcus from Zephyr's house today with Gordo. Sol, his shit is fat! Seriously backyard opens onto the beach, kitchen faces the sea and he has a swimming pool too in case you don't want to walk the extra two hundred feet to the sea! Amazing!"

"Seriously, that sounds dope Rigo. Is it a big house?"

"He said it is four bedroom and six bath. Honestly hermana if you end up in a house like that I'm moving in and Nana too!" He chuckled and I couldn't hold back either. The thought of

Nana running towards the sea first thing in the morning and lounging by the pool was too good to be true but just the thought was enough to make us laugh.

"I'll get that house Rigo, watch. I'll work my ass off and get it for the kids. But maybe I'll go check rent prices in Long Beach first..." I said with a smile. I knew I could find us somewhere and we would adjust. As long as we stayed together and were safe what more could we ask for? A beach house in Malibu... that was the dream, now getting it was the hard part!

CHAPTER EIGHT

Telling the kids about having to move was pretty easy, they reacted with excitement and it dawned on me that maybe too many bad memories cluttered the house for them. They were a little forlorn when they realised they wouldn't have 24 hour access to Nana's house but we determined that coming to visit Nana would be a nice day out and they could always stay the night with her when they wanted to.

Next we turned to the ominous task of packing up everything and figuring out what we could do with the furniture. We decided to leave everything for the moment and headed to the beach with Nana instead.

After spending the day at the beach, the kids decided they were going to stay with Nana so that left me home alone so I turned to my Zephyr movie as a distraction. I was working on their 25 year documentary for their record label who wanted to show it at the party they were hosting and also see if any of the big networks wanted to buy the rights to it for any pieces they decided to feature in honor of their great longevity.

Working on the film was a great escape for me from stress of today but not from the past. Every song and every clip I edited together reminded me of so many concerts, nights out, and my own personal past. Looking at the Zephyr of twenty-five years ago and the one of today was a stark reminder of how I had aged alongside them. Their talents grew from strength to strength over the years and it was as if we had all matured and grown up together. They had had their bad times and their good, and most of what they lived as individuals probably never came out in public and they, like me, were left to suffer alone, without support yet always looking to a brighter future. I was a little nervous about the background track. I had written an eerie melody to use behind my initial montage and was excited to have it featured in such an important short film but I knew it was a risk and chances where I would be asked to replace it with something more mainstream.

I was working with a clip from two years ago of the band hosting a private pool party to raise money for the local children's hospital when I realised the house was the one Rigo had been describing to me. It was really something and all I was looking at was the pool, seaview and backyard! My attention was completely drawn to the house now and the small features that made the house beautiful. I would love to have a house like that, even for a week! The kids would be so happy there and we could have so much fun in a house like that.

Suddenly I had an idea and I scrambled for my calculator and a pad of paper. Numbers were flying onto the page and I was slowly feeling a buzz of excitement in my chest. Maybe I had just stumbled on to a solution. It would take a lot of balls to carry it out but the result would be amazing if it went my way. I didn't need to rely on sex or blackmail to get what I wanted I would merely present a factual proposal and then worry about the long term once I needed to. I could get this project done and then we would have enough money to rent somewhere nice and the money would give me some time to find something suitable for us. But for the short term my plan was coming to fruition. I texted Rigo and told him I needed to speak with him tomorrow and I would explain my plan. I didn't sleep that night thinking about how delightfully crazy my plan was and if it didn't work how we would have a big problem. But if it worked, if I managed to be unabashed and bold for just ten minutes, our life could change and our dream home would be within reach, even if it would be for a short time.

Rodrigo decided to test out his new pancake recipe with the kids the next day and I couldn't wait to tell him my plan.

The kids looked at the pile of pancakes he placed in front of them and with eyes as big as manhole covers they surmounted the quest and once a dozen scrummy peanut butter pancakes had disappeared they ran out of the kitchen towards home, fully fuelled and ready to discover if we could fit all of our things in the treehouse and just live in there.

"So what do you think sis, are they any good?" He looked like a little kid desperate for approval. I had to give him credit he was determined to be a food success story and he was putting so much effort into developing his recipes. I caught him reading Sunset magazine the other day; instead of trying to hide it he started pointing out the great pictures of food and how he could adjust the recipe to add some life and spice to it. His belief was he would be the best chef around because he would 'liven' up the average American food and present a newer, fresher, healthier version. I was just happy to be his taste tester, I am sure I was gaining weight but I was always willing to take a hit for the team... especially if it was a tasty one.

"Rigo, what can I say. Put some Nutella on those and they are the greatest pancakes ever made. Maybe sprinkle some chopped nuts on top.." I mumbled as I finished off the last bite.

"Nutella! You genius!"He grinned wide and I could hear his brain working on how it would look on a plate.

I gulped down the rest of my coffee and wiped my mouth. Feeling like I would roll like a ball for the rest of the day, I pushed my plate away and looked sternly at Rodrigo. I had to convince him of my plan because without his support it would never work.

"Rigo, Listen bro, I have a plan. I think I know where we will go to live."

"Really, is it nearby?" he said still distracted by the prospect of Nutella smothered pancakes.

"Rigo, Listen! You know you were telling me about Marcus D's house? Well I've had an idea."

"Let me guess you are going to break in and just set up house there while he is on tour right!?" He joked and laughed to himself. His smile faded fast when he saw the seriousness in my eyes.

“Sol, you are crazy but please tell me that is not your plan.”

“Not quite, but it is along those lines. I did some math and considering I paid out for eleven studio albums, three b-side albums, countless concert tickets, memorabilia and goodies not to mention their autobiographies and contributions to their favorite charities I figure $5,000 of my money has supported Marcus’s fortune. Without contributions like mine who would these people be?! I figure they owe me. $5,000 is enough to cover one month’s rent right. So I go and present myself there, tell him how much he owes me and then agree to stay in the house for a month while he tours and we look for something else!” I finished excitedly and determinedly.

The look of shock and wonder on Rigo’s face was priceless. He was actually speechless and every time he tried to say something he would stop and try to restart his sentence. I got worried; I had never seen a reaction from him like this before. For the first time the craziness of my idea actually dawned on me and a small amount of doubt creeped into my mind. I quickly dismissed any negativity. The way I saw it the worst that would happen is he would slam the door in my face and say no. Ok, maybe call the cops but no big deal, he says no and I go back to the drawing board. I am sure we could spend a week with Nana; maybe I could get the film done early and we would have more money for a deposit.

"I know it sounds crazy Rigo, but I have nothing to lose and everything to gain. That house is ideal. I can sell it to the kids as like a beach house, I'll finish the film and then we'll get our own beach house. It might be more of a hut then a house but I know it will work. I am due some good karma right?! I've always provided for my kids, I protected them I had the shit kicked out of me and never complained, never asked for help. So.."

"No one is denying you went through hell sis, you haven't had it easy but this is insane! You want your kids to live in a rock star's house?! You know he is on drugs and you know how those people live! Seriously think about it!" He sounded like Nana all of a sudden.

"Marcus is 53 years old, he does a bit of weed but otherwise he is clean living. He had his party days and girls and booze but now he is over that. Love of the music is his life and he is just enjoying being a genius now. Working on music, enjoying the profits of working hard and writing some of the most moving lyrics ever sang!"

"I hear you but I still think this is insane. Why do you need my help then?" he asked me with clear cut annoyance in his voice.

"Because you know where he lives bro! I need you to take me there so I can lay out my plan to him. The way I see it I have nothing to lose Rigo, at this rate and with the money I actually have my options don't really exist. Besides all that, I still owe Xavier money and I have every intention of paying him back every penny." The words sounded heavy, like they were weighted by heartache and burden.

"When did you want to go then?" he asked me glumly.

"The kids are making dinner with Nana tonight so we'll go then. I just pray he is home and we catch him at the right time. Every time I met him before he was so nice and polite. I'm sure this will work Rigo, I am really sure he may just find the whole thing crazy enough that he'll see it as fun. Then it's a win win all around right." I was talking more to myself then to him. I realised just how much I was counting on this man being the same fun loving, witty character I had always met at concerts and interviews.

"Whatever Loca. I'll be here at 6 and we'll go see what happens. I am not getting out of the car though! I am just taking you there and then sitting in the car to wait and if the po po show up you are on your own!" He sounded like a father trying to tell off his wayward daughter.

"Love you Bro, this will work. You'll see" I said as I planted a big kiss on his check as he turned away from me.

The rest of the afternoon passed as it normally would except for the looming stress about the packing and the kid's questions about what was going to happen to us next. They had been through a lot in the last few months and although they never spoke about Brody I knew they had questions. Maybe they'd asked Nana, but they never mentioned his name in front of me; not that I would mind as it would probably be mutually beneficial to talk about him with them.

I wanted to share my plan with them but the more I thought about it the more I realized how crazy it sounded. Could you imagine if every fan that fell on hard times just showed up at their favorite band's house and essentially demanded a refund on their fandom? Bands would be broke if they agreed to that! But some flutter of hope sat inside my chest. I knew these guys, I had met them so many times I was sure Marcus would recognize me.

Years ago I captured a picture of him in full swing belting out his self-professed favorite track. He had tears in his eyes and sweat pouring down his face yet it all mixed up and glistened in the lights. He had his eyes closed like he was in a wonderland of his own and enjoying a moment that was just for him and that song. I found it a really soul bearing image and I kept it for myself. Next time I knew I was going to meet them I had it printed for him and gave it to him privately just in case he didn't like it. When he opened it he was shocked. His face almost melted and his eyes went wet.

"I remember this concert so well. Do you know it was the anniversary of losing my mom and her face popped into my mind and it was like I could hear her singing with me. She had a lovely voice, I can still hear her through my own music sometimes.." He trailed off and stared hard at the picture. I didn't say a word, I just watched his face morph and regain composure, astounded by the personal details he had just shared with me, almost a complete stranger.

“Thanks for this. Soleil isn’t it?” he asked

“Ya, Soleil Di Vittorio. I have more shots I gave to your record label and they asked for some more stuff for your next album, I didn’t give them this one though just because it looks almost like a private moment. I’ll take some more for the label so I’m sure we’ll meet up again.” I stopped talking as I knew I was not saying the right things and blubbering.

“Sounds cool. I really appreciate the picture, you have talent Soliel.” He said a bit wistfully and I knew he was probably thinking about his mom.

“Thanks Marcus, you have a great talent too. You tell stories with your lyrics and reassure people that what they are facing can be sung out loud and the burdens can lessen. You are an inspiration to me, I’ve been a fan since you started singing gigs at Stardust Saloon.” I stopped quickly again, what was wrong with me I couldn’t stop sounding like a little kid!

“Stardust Saloon! My god that was a lifetime ago!” He chuckled.

“You know I’m not such a party boy anymore..” he said quietly.

“Ya I heard, maybe that’s why your music keeps getting better and better though.” I said.

His eyes lifted up and looked right at me. “You are the first person to ever say that to me. Normally I get harassed for not wanting to go party anymore. The music has always been more important; these boys are my brothers and each song is my therapy”

“Well hopefully your life is more important too...” I said thinking of Brody and his steady decline into doom,

We stood there and stared at each other for what felt like ages. He looked at me curiously and it was more like we were both speechless rather than bored. We just held each other’s eyes.

That’s when Brody found me and of course bruises and berating followed as soon as we got home. But I remembered that moment fondly and I had a lot of respect for Marcus and for his integrity and devotion to his music.

I replayed that moment now as I sipped some lemonade on the porch. Maybe the tides would shift for me, maybe I would get a break and the kids and I could enjoy a few weeks of luxury and living as we should. I wanted the best for them and wanted them to love life like I did at that age regardless of the chaos around me.

As if they knew I was thinking of them, the kids appeared from the back of the house. They were flushed and sweaty but always so gorgeous. Jason was chasing his sister and she would slow down to tease him then run away as fast as she could. Her little toothpick legs moving like a roadrunner and her squeals of laughter like a sparkler, delightful and mesmerising all at once.

“Hey guys! Come inside and have a shower! You know Nana doesn’t let smelly kids in her house!” I scolded them with a huge smile.

“We don’t smell Ma, we just have nature’s perfume on!” said Jason matter of factly. Then he ran over and jumped in my lap, helped himself to the rest of my lemonade and rubbed his sweaty brow against my shoulder.

“You have the best lap in the world Ma, Nana is cuddly but you are just comfortable” he declared.

I gave him a big kiss on the head and looked up to see Lily standing there watching us. She was smiling but had a weird look on her face.

“What’s up baby girl? I still have half a lap here waiting for you if you want.”

“I’m okay Ma, I was just thinking how much I will miss the porch when we move. It is like a stage for me and I love sitting on it and watching you sit on that step. Whenever you sit there you look really pretty Ma, and I love to just sit with you and imagine it is a magic porch that will take us on adventures!” she said with renewed excitement in her face.

“Ya, I agree. This porch is definitely magical and the next place we live in will definitely have a magic porch! We will have great adventures!” I responded, praying with all my heart my plan would work and tomorrow I would tell them all about our new digs and our “vacation home”.

CHAPTER NINE

The children had their showers and with dripping hair and hungry bellies they ran over to Nana's for their weekly dinner extravaganza which had now been extended into a pyjama party as Selena was having a movie marathon and needed some company.

Almost immediately there was a knock on the door; I opened it to find a very sombre Rodrigo.

"They kicked me out! Said I tried to take over the dinner preparations! Honestly I was just trying to make sure they didn't burn the garlic otherwise it ruins the whole meal!" he explained with a pout.

"And you think Nana doesn't know this after her 50 years of cooking experience?" I mocked his pout and pulled him inside.

"I'm glad you're here early! Rigo what the hell do I wear?!" I asked, panicked by what I was now set to do.

"Girl you need to flaunt what your mama gave you! Tight, short and tiny will be fine I am sure!" he started twerking and touching himself finding this incredibly amusing.

“Rigo!! Serious dude, help me! I don’t want to sleep with him, I just need to convince him to agree with my version of crazy! What do you wear to go and ask someone if they will take your fandom as payment for rent in their own house!? I am seriously crazy bro... what was I thinking?!”

“You ain’t backing out now! I got money on the cops showing up before you even get your name out of your mouth!” He chuckled and carried on twerking in front of the mirror.

“Fuck you Rigo, this plan will work, call it the cosmos but I have a good feeling about this! Fuck it I’ll wear my butterfly print summer dress with some sandals and tie my hair up, that will work well and kind of stays middle right? I’m not going there to ho myself so that outfit will work, right?” I glanced over at Rigo who was now fixated on my fridge and the lack of substance on my shelves.

“Yo, do you even feed your kids man? What kind of a fridge is this, no wonder they practically ate my hand off when I offered them cookies! Dude, go shopping or something! You can’t carry on...”

His words trailed off as I walked further down the hallway. Yes, the outfit, the plan it would all work and by the end of the week we would be moved into a million dollar home on the beach. It would work, I had a good feeling about this, I just prayed it wasn't false hope and he wouldn't even be there.

About twenty minutes later I emerged in a cloud of perfume and determination. I looked good, not great or sexy but modest, just as I wanted to; this was business at the end of the day, business.

"Let's go freak, I'm ready!" I barked at Rigo in my most determined voice.

"What no please? Seriously you going like that, no makeup, hair pulled back? You look like a teacher that is coming to scold a pupil. Loosen up a bit or you will just scare him, you are already scarring me!" He did a fake shudder and smiled.

"Seriously, should I let my hair down, does that make me less intimidating?" I asked.

"That would be a good start! Cover your neck up too Sol, there is still a bruise there, don't want him getting wind of all that shit now right? Come on, let's go. Traffic won't be good at this time and we have to cross LA to go visit your prince and secure your castle. Lucky man landing you..." he didn't finish his sentence as the kick I delivered hurt too much.

“I’m not going there to seduce him idiot, how many times do I need to tell you that?! He has a soon to be empty house on the beach and will need a house sitter. You see it’s a mutually beneficial relationship.” I said most assuredly.

“Ok, ok. I was just playing. You look pretty Sol, just be careful. Men can be dogs and I don’t want this punk to take advantage of you or hurt the kids. After everything you have been through this isn’t the perfect solution but I guess we don’t have many options, especially as you won’t take the money and I offered and just stay put” he lamented.

“Aw bro, I’ll miss you too and tell you what, if this doesn’t work out then I’ll take the money off you and stay put ok. But I’m going to pay you back and I definitely do not want to know where you get it from ok?!” I conceded.

“You serious! That would be amazing! I’ll sort it out Sol promise. You can work the van for free to pay me back as I’ll need some extra hands.” He was so happy I thought he would cry.

“Ok, well lets go try my plan first, Malibu beach or stinking taco van..uumm let me see....” I joked. We made our way to the car jumped in and set off west for the place I was hoping would soon be home.

The evening was breezy and beautiful. The sun was starting to set and I was so happy Rigo took his convertible. I shook out my hair and we drove in silence just happy with the moment and the wonderful feeling of the warm wind, gorgeous sun and safe company. The traffic wasn't too bad and we got to Malibu as the sun was inching its way into the sea. Without asking Rigo pulled up and turned the car off sitting in silence with his face determinedly turned towards the setting sun, we watched the effortless glide of the lamp of the world dancing off into the horizon; I said a silent prayer and felt refreshed. As the last speck disappeared for another day Rigo grabbed my hand and we just looked at each other.

"I'll get you the money Soleil, you don't have to do this" he whispered.

"I think I do Rigo, if this works we could have an amazing time and the kids would be so happy. It would be like a dream come true. Let's see what the world has in my kismet, like I said if he says no then I'll work the taco van with a smile and stay. But I feel like a need to try, I need to be bold again, determined again and being that close to the band will make my film amazing. I could really be onto a success here... I just want to try.." I looked away and drew in a deep breath.

Rodrigo started the car again and we were off, the air was a bit sharper now that the sun had gone but I felt a warmth from inside, I felt guided and confident an adventure was about to begin.

The next thing I realised, Rigo is turning off the main road towards the sea. We started slowly down a red brick and gravel path, once we rounded the corner there was what looked like a glass and stone mirage painted against the darkening sky. Lights reflected in the glass and the bricks looked lilac and warm, almost exhausted from the heat of the day and now glowing with relief for the night. You couldn't see much of the house because they had cleverly fronted it with a huge garage but you could hear the sea crashing and smell the salt in the air. This house was so set back from neighbors and the main road it seemed almost forgotten, as though it served as a bubble of fantasy in the hectic LA scene and would allow you to enter and disappear from the rush and rigor of the world. Lights were on already and shinning dimly through the few windows that faced out towards the driveway. I was amazed there was no gate although I am sure there were cameras everywhere. My heart started racing more out of desire than anything else. This was a dream, this was what I had always wanted and seeing something so beautiful perched above the glorious beaches and sea of Malibu only steeled my determination to at least try and get a bit of my own regardless how unconventional it seemed.

"This is it sis, like I said, I'm not coming with you but I'll sit in the car and wait for the 5-0 to show up, ok?" Rodrigo said with a wink.

"It's beautiful isn't it? Imagine this is where you wake up every day, it's a dream. So much better then I imagined" I said quietly as the natural sounds deserved respect and I didn't want to disturb the beauty all around me.

"Lights are on, so that's a good sign. Can you go already? You have at least four minutes before anything fun happens out here so you should go try out your plan you crazy nut!" he cajoled.

"Ya, you're right. Let's get this over with and see what is written for me today." I stepped out of the car and took in a few deep breaths closing the car door gently behind me.

"Your hair looks better now too.." he chuckled and slouched a bit further down his seat.

I started walking towards the house and noticed immediately a shadow moving across one of the windows moving towards the solid wooden door. I was about a yard away from the doorbell when the door was flung open and a German Shepard appeared in the empty space. It was growling very quietly and the sound filled me with dread. I don't mind dogs but I can't imagine anyone likes being attacked by one, so I stopped dead in my tracks. Suddenly I noticed a hand holding back the dog and slowly a face appeared from behind the door. It was Marcus himself, he looked angry, disturbed and slightly confused.

"Who are you?" he growled still not pulling the dog away.

Swallowing the biggest lump in my throat and fighting the dryness in my mouth I managed to whisper "Hi Marcus, my name is Soleil."

"I'm not here on that kind of business, I just got one of your friends to bring me here because I wanted to see you and ask you something." I said shyly. This was not going to plan, my confidence had gone and I was sounding like an awestruck fan who wanted to just admire a rockstar and giggle like an idiot.

"Look you obviously are a fan and want an autograph or something right? Fucking Gordo, I knew he would start cashing in on our dealings." He muttered to himself but looking at me like he knew me and remembered my face.

I stood up straight again, looked straight at Marcus and with determination said "No you have it all wrong. Yes this is a bit crazy and yes Gordo is how I found out about this place but actually he doesn't know I am here and as far as dealing anything I don't do that, I came to speak to you about something. A business idea and maybe something that is mutually beneficial in the end. We've met properly before Marcus, a few years ago before you gave a concert at El Colombo. I gave you a picture you said reminded you of your mom."

He didn't reply straight away and stared at me. I found it a bit awkward especially when a smile came over his face and he very obviously relaxed. His whole face changed and his eyes sparkled with joy as he pulled the dog back inside and came out closing the door behind him.

"Soleil, isn't it? Sorry I don't remember your last name." he said quietly.

"Di Vittorio. Do you still have the picture?" I asked eagerly.

"Come round the back with me and we'll go in through the deck instead, saves me having to deal with the dog." He started off down a stone path alongside the house that looked like it would eventually go straight into the sea.

"I am sorry to bother you, this place is amazing and so beautiful. You don't hear anything except the sea and the birds and what a place to wake up and take in every day." I gushed because I was nervous.

"It's my sanctuary, my bit of peace in the world. Some people buy islands, I bought this and try to be here as much as possible. Watch your step now, I just watered the plants so it might be wet."

I was shocked how normal he was being, he seemed to have relaxed completely and it felt like he didn't mind I had just intruded on his property and time. He opened a sliding glass door which led us into a plush living room. The couches were all brown leather and covered with multicolored cushions. You could see this was a well-used room as there were magazines strewn about and books on the side tables. Fur hides covered some of the seats and it was such a lovely and welcoming room. When I turned around to close the door, I realised we were now facing the sea and I could vaguely see the waves continuous dance towards the shore. It took my breath away and I stood frozen starring out over the clifftop, taking in the view and also the swimming pool that seemed to spill over into the sea.

“Nice view huh? There is a beach down there but because of the cliff you can’t see it until you are over it.” He interrupted my thoughts and dragged me back into the moment.

“Come in, shut the door, I want to show you something.” He strode confidently into the next room.

I hesitated, thinking about what I was doing. I had no idea what Marcus was up to and now I was on my own, in his house, blindly following him deeper into the house, however, I couldn’t help but enjoy the moment because the house was everything I could have ever dreamed of. It was richly decorated but still welcoming, it drew you in and there were glass walls and high ceilings adorned with exotic pieces that showed the travel savviness of its owner. The house was completely open planned and I caught a glimpse of the kitchen through the gap next to the fireplace.

"You coming?" he said slightly impatiently. I hurried towards his voice and realised maybe he had company or I was actually disturbing him at work on something important. I felt like an idiot all of a sudden and moved a bit faster as I was feeling more like a nuisance then anything.

I walked into the next living room and found him gazing up at the wall. I followed his gaze and couldn't believe my eyes! My picture was enlarged and framed up on his wall. The look on his face hadn't changed and the picture almost captured an ethereal glow around his head as if his mother had been standing behind him just at that moment.

"I would never forget this picture, I love it so much. It's like you captured me completely vulnerable yet strong all at the same time. I still remember when you gave it to me, you were so timid but I also remember what you said about my music that day too and now that you are here I guess I just wanted to say thank you. This picture means a lot to me and is one of the only things I kept from the thousands of pictures, trinkets and paintings I get from fans so it is only right to thank you properly." He was staring straight at me with a smile, I felt timid again.

No matter how old he got Marcus was always so handsome. With sun-kissed curly locks tumbling low on his forehead and bright blue eyes scanning his surroundings, he stood tall and broad with a solid build and always so well dressed. I never crushed on him but I was never blind to how gorgeous he was and how his calmness only enhanced every feature and drove women crazy.

"Wow, I didn't really expect you to like it so much. I thought maybe I was the only one who saw the beauty of the picture and how it just seemed to catch you in almost a spiritual light. When you mentioned your mom it made sense, it seems like she was there and that is what you can see glowing all around you." I stopped as I realised I was off track from my mission and talking about some very personal things with a man I had just intruded on and still had to ask if we could move into this piece of paradise!

"I didn't think anyone else saw that, and no one who has seen it up here on the wall has ever described it like that. I totally agree with you, I love it. Seriously. I love it and I want to thank you for it. It brings me a lot of comfort and I can't imagine not having it. So thank you." He looked deep into my eyes and smiled. He had a beautiful smile and his face glowed with knowledge and self-contentment that was reassuring and mesmerising all at the same time.

"Soleil, not to be rude or change gears but can I ask what the hell brought you here tonight? I mean it's nice to get to thank you in person for the picture but in all honesty I was not expecting you to show up and definitely not through my connection with Gordo." He said as he fell into a comfy looking armchair and never taking his eyes off me.

"Please sit down, sorry where are my manners. Can I get you a drink?" he asked.

I sat down opposite him on an equally comfy armchair, "No thanks I'm ok. I won't take up too much of your time and I just want to say thank you for even letting me in. I know this seems crazy and the only way I know Gordo is because he lives down the road from me and I've known him most of his life. Like I said he doesn't know I'm here and this has nothing to do with weed or anything like that."

“Yes you mentioned a business proposal so I’ll tell you what. As repayment for the picture, I’ll listen to it and we’ll see what happens after that, shall we?” he answered. His mouth curled into a smile again and it seemed he was very amused by this odd series of events transpiring.

“Ok I’ll just say it then. I have been a massive fan of Zephyr since you started. I followed you even before you were Zephyr and I have always thought your lyrics are genius and the guys who play behind you are the most amazing musicians alive. I have bought every album you ever made, the mainstream and b-sides sometimes even having to buy the cassette and then the CD. I went to as many concerts as I could and always bought t-shirts and all sorts of stuff. I even donated to your charity just because I believed in your work and your music has always been so important to me.” This was it, this was why I had come.

“You sound like you want a refund or something. Did the last album let you down?” he asked with a chuckle.

I stared straight at him and almost froze. All I could think was this is insane.

“Well... maybe in a weird way I am...” I muttered.

"What! Are you fucking kidding me? Is this a joke? You want a refund for all the money you invested in us because the last album wasn't up to your liking!?" He was sitting up straight now and the smile had gone.

"No, that's not what I mean. I love the last album and love how timeless your lyrics are but... no.. well can I just explain." I was getting flustered now and doubting my confidence.

"Please do, because this sounds fucking ridiculous and outrageous!" He said sternly.

"Ok, well, you remember the guy who was with me when I gave you the picture, well that was my other half. I kicked him out about a month ago and haven't heard anything since. I have two kids and last week our landlord came and told me that we are behind on rent and I owe over five grand to him next week or I need to get out. So I guess you could say I am homeless, slightly broke and looking for a miracle." I started.

Marcus visibly relaxed and sat back into his chair. "What does any of this have to do with me?" he asked.

"Well I figure, five grand is about what I spent on the band over the years and I know this sounds crazy but I was thinking maybe, especially as I know you have a tour coming up and stuff... well, maybe.. maybe we could make an arrangement where I could come stay here while you tour and house sit for you? We could count the five grand as a prepaid rent and then we all win in the end." I stopped, having now said it and heard it for myself, I realised that no one would ever agree to such a plan.

"I'm sorry, I shouldn't have come here, or asked. You don't know me yet I'm asking you to let me and my kids come stay in this amazing house just because I've been a loyal fan. I'm sorry Marcus, forgive the intrusion. I'll get out of your way, so sorry, I don't know what I was thinking." I stood up, defeated, he didn't need to say anything, I knew this was silly and I actually felt embarrassed for even asking and ashamed of taking advantage of Rigo and even intruding on this man's life in the slightest.

I was trying to figure out the way back to the door to make a quick exit, hold back tears and still berating myself when he interrupted me.

"Wow, you have some serious balls! You come to my house with my dealer, and within ten minutes of being in the house, you tell me you want to live in this house! You know how much this is worth? I have worked my ass off to find this little piece of quiet and you think kids and a woman are going to let me enjoy it the way I like to enjoy it? I live on my own with Dani and we just get on with life, I have never had kids in this house and I definitely haven't ever had a roommate!" He was standing now too and walking towards me. I was looking for anger but was surprised when I saw the bemused look on his face.

"You want to house sit for me while I go on tour? I leave a stranger in my house for minimum a month and let her and her kids take over the place?" He asked again.

"Yes, that is what I asked. I'm sorry, I didn't realise how crazy and desperate that sounds. It has just been a hard time for us lately and I thought maybe I was due some good luck and trying something crazy was a good idea. I am so sorry. Please forget I asked or came and I'll just get out of here." I hung my head and turned away.

The whole house went silent, only in the far distance could I hear the waves and the call of the sea. A place like this was a dream for someone like me and Rigo was right, I was just being crazy for even thinking this plan would work. It was so quiet and calm all of a sudden, I thought Marcus had left the room. I turned around and he was still there, staring at me with a bewildered look on his face.

"Listen, like I said you have a lot of nerve to come here and ask to move in purely because you have been a devoted fan. But I tell you what, I respect guts and I have had hard times hit me too. I guess not having kids makes taking the hit easier but I'm still human and from a person to person level it seems like you have had a tough time. You obviously have talent and you are confident so I imagine your kids must be pretty cool too." He paused and drew in a deep breath.

"I can't believe I'm saying this but maybe it would be nice to have some company for a bit and know Dani is looked after properly while I'm away. Maybe we could try this out for a few weeks and see how it goes..." he deliberately trailed off.

His words hit me like a bus. Was he agreeing? Was I hearing this right?

"Sorry, what did you say? Are you serious?" I asked in a state of shock.

"Ya, why not? You did something nice for me a long time ago and of course fan support is what built this place so why not? I can go with crazy for a little while. I mean we can try this out and see what happens right?" he shrugged his shoulders and broke out into a deep laugh.

"Maybe with kids around I won't feel so old!" He laughed again.

This gorgeous, world famous icon had just agreed to try out my crazy plan. I was in shock, I couldn't hide it. This house would be our retreat, our roof until we got our own beachside house. I couldn't believe it.

"Marcus, are you for real? Me, kids, stuff all come here and we all stay here? You are cool with that?"

"You must have thought it possible if you came out here to ask. It will go down as one of the craziest things I've ever done but to hell with it. Crazy is what got me this far! When did you want to move in?" he asked so casually.

"By next week?" I couldn't believe this was going to happen, but there was no way I was going to mess this up now he was agreeing to let us stay.

"Ok, well you obviously know where I live and I do enjoy privacy so could you come after Thursday in the evening so that not everyone sees you show up with all your stuff please?" He was a cool as could be, it was like he was arranging for furniture to be delivered.

“Of course, we’ll be discreet and we haven’t got that much to be honest. I am a bit surprised, I can’t thank you enough. I have always dreamed of a house like this and for my kids to wake up to the beach everyday even for a month would be a dream come true. Honestly I am so grateful. You won’t even know we are here and I’ll buy all my own food and cleaning stuff you won’t have to worry about anything. I can cook and clean too and I promise we won’t be a bother at all.”

“I’m sure we’ll figure it all out, I’m not sure why I am agreeing to this but let’s try it out right? Who knows what will happen and I won’t be here much because of the new album we are working a lot so ya... I guess it’s just cool to be able to help out a fellow wonderer...” he said staring right at me and smiling.

“Fellow wonderer? Ya I guess you could say that.. Look I know most women who come here are normally here for your amusement or trying to win your love, I just want to be clear that I’m here on a totally platonic basis. I absolutely love your music and think you’re cool but I hope you don’t think I’m like a groupie trying to get in here and seek fame and fortune off your back. I just want to housesit and finish a big project I have on at the moment which once I sell it will help us get out of your hair."

"No disrespect Soleil, but you are not the type of girl I normally bring back home or find 'amusement' with. Like you said this is a mutually beneficial arrangement and I will respect you and your kids and I hope we will at least be friends." He winked and stuck out his hand for a shake.

I shook his hand and relaxed because it felt so welcoming, so soft and warm. This might just work, his face was searching, his eyes piercing mine, trying to learn something, anything but unable to see a glimmer of light.

"Great, well I'll leave now and see you next week Thursday. Thank you again Marcus and thanks for seeing past the craziness of it all. You were really cool about everything, even me just showing up like this." I said as I noticed he was still holding my hand, so I took it back and walked towards the front door.

"Ah no worries, I actually have the police on speed dial and was ready to call them before you mentioned the picture. I'll see you Thursday and I'm looking forward to meeting your kids." He said as he opened the front door and spied Rigo in the car.

"Your body guard?" he asked.

"No just my brother, Gordo's friend. Thanks again, I'll see you Thursday then!" I walked off towards the car as Rigo turned on the engine.

I jumped over the door and slid in the seat next to him beaming from ear to ear.

"No Way! He agreed to your hare-brained scheme! The feds didn't show so I figured it was cool" he said animatedly.

"He said yes Rigo, we are moving in next Thursday! I can't believe it! That house, that view oh man wait till the kids see it!! Things are looking better by the day Rigo, better by the day!"

CHAPTER TEN

With sun pouring through my window like a yellow brick road, I woke up to the freshest feeling of success and anticipation I had felt in a long time. I jumped up and got ready, I couldn't wait to get over to Nana's to tell her and the kids about our new lodgings and the amazing adventure we were about to embark on. I realised there was a flutter in my stomach again, I was still in a state of shock that Marcus had agreed but now there was so much to do to make this a reality. I looked around at the furniture and curtains we had painstakingly accumulated the kitchen table we had sat around and shared memories with. All of a sudden everything had no value. I didn't want to take any of this with me, it was baggage, reminders and most significantly the past. There would be no need to move any of these things, no reason to hold on to these possessions which had a shared history with us. I was ready to move on from everything, seize this beautiful opportunity and make new memories. I wanted a new life, no baggage, no stigmas or painful reminders. This was a chance for me to start again, from next Thursday onwards it was me and the kids, journeying together and making life what we wanted it to be. Time to start planning a garage sale!

I walked out the front door into the sunshine and skipped along to Nana's house opening the door to the luscious smell of breakfast and five different giggles. No one heard me creep in and walk right up to the kitchen door as they were too busy laughing and all looking in the same direction. When I finally looked around the door, I soon added my own laughter to the furore. Standing at the stove was Rodrigo, in Nana's pink apron and his Pink Panther boxer shorts doing his usual lip sync and twerk to the song blasting out of the radio. He knew everyone was laughing but he had no care in the world, he was in his element and between the terrible singing voice and bad taste in clothes it was amazing he kept a straight face.

"Ma! Look at Tio! He already did Britney now he's trying to do a Beyonce song!" Lily squealed with delight and fell into a fresh fit of giggles.

Selena got up and threw her arms around her brother and started singing alongside him. They did an impromptu dance routine and by that time Nana was crying she was laughing so hard. Jason was sitting at the table clapping his hands and smiling ear to ear singing along with the radio at the top of his lungs. I stood there and drank up the scene before me, the happiness, craziness and laughter was what I wanted to take with me, to keep hold of and cherish. All of these moments were priceless and meant more to me than any piece of furniture or decoration. This is what I have always held on to, held memories tight and when I needed comfort let them resurface and play out in my mind again.

Rigo turned around at that moment and saw me standing in the doorway and smiled, he hip bumped Selena and winked at her to follow his lead as he moved towards me. Selena read his mind and they both surrounded me serenading me and twerking up a storm. The singing got louder and even more off key but my laughing became uncontrollable, especially when Nana got up and started doing her version of twerking without a care in the world. This colorful and mad scene lasted until the song finished and then the music abruptly stopped; Jason had turned off the radio.

"Ok, now that you guys have had fun can I have some breakfast please I am starving!!!" he said with a very serious look on his face.

We all had one last chuckle and Selena gave me a big hug before she went off to her bedroom. Rigo went back to the stove and within seconds had a plateful of French toast in front of Jason.

"Will that be enough for you, Sir?" he joked.

"Hey Tio! What about me!?" squealed Lily.

"You? Oh ya, forgot about you and your love for cinnamon... I guess Ma will have to wait for the next batch as these special cinnamon swirl toast are all for you princess!" he said lovingly while she clapped her hands and her eyes went wide.

"Mija you have a twinkle in your eye. What has brought this on then?" asked Nana suspiciously.

"Nana how do you always know something is up? It's like you have super mind reading powers or something!" I retorted with a smile.

"I do, I also have a grandson who can't keep a secret for longer than 30 minutes!" she joked.

"Rigo! You let the cat out of the bag already?!" I asked with a fake pout as I knew he would have told Nana already.

"Yes Nana, kids I have some great news! I have found us a new place to live temporarily until I finish my Zephyr project and find us a permanent place. It's a great house right by the beach and it has a swimming pool!" I explained to three sets of eyes that were growing bigger and wider by the second.

"A swimming pool Ma?!" Jason shrieked.

"By the beach?!" Lily whispered in shock.

"Yes and yes!" I said as I rushed forward and planted a kiss on their heads and playfully stole a bite of cinnamon toast from Lily's plate.

"We are going to housesit for someone very special and enjoy the life of kings this summer! We can move in next Thursday! We have so much to do in the meantime so hurry up and eat we need to plan a garage sale!" I was so excited I failed to notice the dark cloud pass in front of Nana's face before she blew.

"You are insane Soleil! You are not taking these kids to a stranger's house to 'house sit' like a bunch of vagabonds! What happens when it doesn't work anymore and the owner wants you out?! Where will you go? You haven't thought about this at all have you and now you want me to be happy that you are taking the kids to basically jump off a cliff into nothing?!" She was shouting now and had stood up and put a protective arm around Jason.

"You made bad choices already Soleil, you took chances and they got you into this mess. You think being stupid and crazy is going to get you anywhere now? You can not treat these kids like luggage and try to make it all better with your pool and beach when you have no idea where you will be in a month! No, you are not doing it. Rigo and the boys will put everything in storage for you and then you come stay here, finish your project and then find a place of your own!" she carried on muttering things in Spanish under her breath.

"Nana, listen, I have thought this through. We are not staying with a complete stranger, I know the owner and we worked together before. This is temporary, yes, and I have not gone mad. I just wanted to find a wonderful place to stay for a while and I have! How dare you accuse me of endangering the kids! You think every problem is solved by moving into this house?! You don't have all the answers Nana, you just have your opinions. I'm on my own now and I am going to make damn sure that my kids get the best of the best! They are not going to grow old in the barrio and aspire to be nothing but another Gordo or Juan driving around dealing and dying!" I sat myself firmly in an empty chair at the table avoiding Lily and Jason's faces but holding Nana's glare.

I lowered my voice before I continued “ Nana, this is not ideal. I know this. The kids have already lost their dad and now we are losing our home. What else can I do? We could stay here but that isn’t ideal is it? Not for you or anyone else that lives here. Nana, Marcus is a really nice person, sincere and willing to help us. I haven’t gone into this blind and trust me if there was another way I would take that option but I don’t see how I am going to get my project done here and that house is in a great place, it will inspire me to do such an amazing job and all the while the children will be safe and happy. Isn’t that the most important thing?” I folded my hands on the table and looked up at Nana, just catching a glisten in her eye as she looked away and started addressing the fridge.

“Fine. You have survived you whole life on your instincts Mija, you do what you have to do. I’m not happy about this one bit but I’m not your mother or your father and you have to do what you think is best for you and the kids. So explain more to me, help me understand. Who is Marcus, where is this place?” she said quietly but sternly.

Instinctively I got up and went to give Nana a big hug. Rodrigo patted my back as I passed him and then turned back to his cooking. I could feel the kid's eyes on my back and almost hear the million questions buzzing in their heads but too afraid to come out. Nana accepted my hug begrudgingly and forced a small smile but I knew she would never accept or understand what I had done.

"Okay, Okay" she said pushing me away. "Sit down and eat. This pink idiot should have something made for you by now."

I sat down next to Lily as she looked at me with a very anxious look on her face. Rigo, put a plate of French toast in front of me and sat opposite with eyes on me too.

"You all want more details now or should I eat first?! Honestly, I feel like an animal in the zoo!"

I got no response just further stares so I knew food would have to wait.

"You are moving into Zephyr's house??! In Malibu?!" I heard in a shriek from behind me. Selena had come back in and caught the last bit of the conversation.

"Soleil, are you serious?! How did you do that?! I am so coming with you!" she was almost giddy.

"Thank you Selena, I appreciate the support and encouragement. Of course you will come over once we settle in and the tour starts." I felt relieved that someone was happy and excited. The kids had still not said a word and were now staring at their plates with worried looks on their faces.

"What's up kids? I know this is a bit weird but trust me, the house is amazing and you are about to have the best summer ever! Trust me, it is going to be so much fun!" I said in my happiest tone, hoping to snap them out of their deflated stares.

"Ma, are you serious? Marcus from Zephyr wants us to live with him?! Wow! Is he your boyfriend now Ma?" asked Jason very quietly.

"He is definitely not my boyfriend Jason, but he has offered to help us out and he needs help looking after the place as he is really busy with his upcoming tour and promoting their new album." I spoke directly to him and made him look me in the eyes as I told him as I wanted the situation to be clear and understandable for the kids.

"Ma?" Lily whispered "What if Daddy wants to find us again? He won't know where we are and he'll get angry again?"

I stopped mid-bite and starred at Lily in shock. I didn't mean to make her feel uneasy but this was the first time she had mentioned Brody and I couldn't work out if she was missing him or scared of him.

"What do you mean baby? Do you want Daddy to come back to live with us?" I asked her gently.

"No Ma, I don't miss Daddy anymore, I don't want him to hurt you anymore that is all. If he comes home and we are gone he will get angry and if I think about it I get scared" she explained still looking down at her hands.

"Don't worry about Daddy, Princess, if he shows up I'll be here and I'll make sure he isn't angry anymore" reassured Rigo as he patted her head and looked at me with head shaking.

"Lily, Jason... I love you two so much. I will always do whatever I think is right for both of you and I will also do my best to make sure you have an amazing life. Staying in Malibu will be like a vacation for us, we'll have fun every day, we'll be safe and before you know it we will have a new house where you can both have your own rooms and you won't have to worry about anyone hurting me. Marcus is super excited to meet you both and he is so happy we will look after his dog while he is away. Everyone is really happy about this guys, there is no need to worry about it and if we go and you two are genuinely not happy then we will come back and stay with Nana ok?" The words just gushed out of me, the fact that I knew Lily often thought of Brody and his destruction brought back so much emotion to me and I didn't want to cry in front of them. I had to be strong and confident in this plan if anyone else was going to believe me.

CHAPTER ELEVEN

The saying goes 'time flies' but in truth it absolutely sped away! Xavier came over to see what was going to happen on Wednesday the day of our garage sale, so I gave him as much cash as I had managed to get together plus I borrowed some from Rodrigo just because I wanted to leave our old house with good karma and I still had every intention of paying Xavier every penny he was owed. You could see sadness in his face and surprise when I gave him the envelope with the money. He walked around the house, examined our wares on display for sale and had a good look around the garden. I was pricing up some books when he found me in the family room.

"Mija, I want a word.." he said quietly.

"No problem, let me just finish closing this box." I replied wincing at the screech of the tape as the roll finished, "what can I do for you?" I asked cheerily turning my full attention to him. He looked solemn and it looked like he had something heavy on his chest.

"I want to thank you for looking after the place so well. It actually feels like a home and even the garden looks great" he started looking very somber.

"You are very brave Soleil, I have great respect for you and how you have held everything together so well even when your heart was breaking and times seemed dark for you" he said staring at me directly in the eyes.

"Thank you Xavier, you have been amazing too, its like a partnership I guess, but it was always good to know if something went wrong you came round and made it good again without any question" I replied, accepting that Xavier had been as good to us as we had been to the house, it had been a mutual respect.

"Well than it should not be a surprise to you if I tell you that I care a lot for you and the kids and that is why you are going to take this money back as a gift from me, not as your landlord but as your Tio. Take it and take care, I pray the Almighty keeps you well and protects the children" he finished with tears in his eyes.

"No way Xavier, that is not right. Brody denied you what was rightfully yours and you run this as a business so you must take it!" I couldn't believe what he was saying to me.

"Listen! I took the money as your landlord but now I am giving it to you as your uncle so no questions and no debate. You will need this money and just because Brody is a waste don't think for a minute I see you with those same eyes" he said sternly.

I had no words, mentioning Brody, giving me money that I knew would help and leaving my lovely home was all too much. I hugged Xavier and sobbed on his shoulder and he held me firmly, without any uncomfortableness. It felt like I had a dad for the first time, a protector, someone who was going to help me, never hurt me. I didn't want to let go but eventually Xavier unpeeled himself, straightened his tie and held me at arm's length by the shoulders regaining his composure and drying his eyes.

"Mija, be happy, find happy somewhere and keep going. Joy and love are waiting for you somewhere, so go and don't give up on the world; it owes you so much more." He said ever so softly.

The last two tears I would allow streamed down my cheeks and I stood there in shock. I couldn't believe this man was offering me such kindness and respect. I felt a surge of hope, as if this was a sign of good things to come and validation I was doing the right thing.

"Shall I carry this out to the trailer for you Mija?" he asked as he picked up a box and hid his face.

"Nah, Tio, we are not going til tomorrow so it can wait." I replied. "Gracias Tio, you don't know how much your words mean to me." I smiled at him as he put the box down and looked at me again.

"I wish you all the best Soleil, and I'll come visit Nana when I need an update on your new lavish life" he joked. He left quite quickly and I heard him shout out his goodbyes to the kids as he walked to his car.

I stashed the money in my purse and smiled as it would be so good to have a little money to support us properly and put towards our new home. The excitement was uncontainable, I felt so full of life again, so excited for tomorrow and all the wonder it would bring. It would be awkward for all of us, I know moving into a world famous rock star's house was not something you did everyday but I also knew that that evening I visited Marcus, he had been genuinely relaxed about it, he had given me no reason to worry.

I walked back out into the front garden; the boys had taken all the furniture out of the house and moved it on to the driveway. They thought it was hilarious as they reconstructed the family room outside and were sitting on the couches chilling like they would do normally! All our little bits were priced out and on display; Lily and Jason were making last checks and looked very professional with Lily toting a clipboard around and Jason in charge of the money box. We had hung out signs all over the neighbourhood to invite people to come, we had been officially 'open' for about half an hour but so far no one showed up. I was silently praying that everything would sell, I didn't feel attached to anything we had priced up and I had nothing but dread when I thought about having to put things in storage or take to Goodwill. We were one day away from a new start, the most unconventional of starts but a start all the same and I wanted to leave as much baggage behind as possible.

All of a sudden a large crowd appeared walking towards our house headed by the familiar shape of Nana. She had a beaming smile on her face and looked like she was leading the 4th of July parade! I started laughing at the sight and shouted out to the kids "you better be ready and look smart kids, Nana is here with her church ladies!" They strode up the road and all the boys stood to attention for their mothers, aunties and grandmothers some with looks of dread as they knew they would soon be employed as mules to get the women's goodies home!

The ladies descended on the garage sale and soon there was a loud buzz of laughter and chat interlaced with excellent bargaining and heckling. Jason was struggling to keep up with the money flying in at him and was grateful for the constant shouts of "keep the change" as his mental maths were well and truly being tested! I started to realise that for small items $20 bills were being passed over, some women didn't even take an item just handed over big hugs and bills to the kids. Nana turned and looked at me beaming, I walked towards her with wide eyes.

"Nana, they aren't buying anything that costs that much. What are they doing?" I asked with genuine surprise.

"The church decided to send you off with something, we told everyone donations for this week can be made to you and the kids. Everyone will miss you Soleil, you made such a big impact on our community and never asked for anything.

We love you, we will all miss you and we spent all morning praying for you mija. We pray God will bless you forever."

I gave her a massive hug and thanked her, I knew she had made this happen and now with a little stash from Xav and this we would be able to set up home sooner rather than later! I just had to give some of the money back to Rigo and then we would have like $10,000 to start fresh once our month at Marcus' was over, the day was brighter already.

I was completely oblivious that Lupe had come up to stand next to me. Lupe was my neighbour from across the road, she was raising three kids on her own and we often shared a drink and a chat on one of our porches late at night when calm had finally descended on the houses. I looked at her and smiled, "This is it Lupe, the day is here, you want anything? Take some toys for the kids!"

"Ya, I want to buy your couch Sol, how much you want for it?" she asked moodily.

"For you...$80...what do you think?... I will even get the boys to take it over and set it up for you." I answered jovially.

"I don't want it in my house, I want it in the backyard on the patio so we can hang out outside this summer. I'll give you $400 for it." She said without even blinking an eye.

"$400!! You must be crazy girl, no way. I said $80! You deaf?!" I said shocked.

"Sol, you gunna take my $400 and when you make it big you come back and pay me back my $320 ok. I never forgot what you did for Miklo, $400 ain't shit compared to that. If I had lost him Sol, I would have lost my soul, you know this, you understand what I am saying, how it feels. I saved up a little something and I want you to have it, treat the kids, take them to Disneyland or something, but take it. I want you to make it Sol, you and me we survive, our kids are fucking soldiers. We will end up on the up Sol, you know this, I know this, we just need the rest of the world to catch up and realize."

I stared deep into her eyes and felt the same connection I felt that day we almost lost Miklo. He had been playing in the front yard as usual and Rigo and I were sat on the porch shooting the shit and Miklo was roughly in our sights. This car pulled up outside Lupe's house and some strange guy was in the driver's seat. It looked like he was talking to Miklo and trying to get him to come to the car. I slapped Rigo on the shoulder and our eyes met, we knew what to do. We got up and sprinted silently towards the car just as the man was opening the passenger side door of the car. I ran in front of the car and sprinted towards the house, grabbing Miklo under my arm. I heard shouting and Rigo swearing. I got to the door and shouted for Lupe, she came running and I gave her Miklo and told her to call the cops. Our eyes had locked then and she knew instantly what had happened. That night she called me from across the street and I went over. We cracked a bottle of Cisco and talked till late at night, when I left we were bonded, I knew I had a friend for life.

"Lupe, you are amazing, honestly, that day with Miklo was saving my own kids, you don't owe me shit for that. I love you like a sister girl and I am gunna miss you so much. Promise you save a seat for me on the couch right. I am gunna come back and tell you all about the new place and all my movie star friends!" She looked at me and we started laughing hysterically.

We spent the rest of the day packing, cleaning and just doing little things to leave our home as we loved it. Nana was hosting a party for us at her place and soon it looked like the whole neighbourhood were there and the smell of BBQ invited us to come over. Every single thing we had put out for sale went, most for an exaggerated price we took as a gift each time and I was astounded how generous every person was. It was such a massive relief to know I had about $10,000 cash with me now. Whatever happened in the next week would happen but at least I had enough to get a hotel or something if the worst ever happened. Life lesson, always secure a roof; No matter what, get a roof; especially with kids in tow.

I woke up the next morning with the dawn chorus ringing in my ears. I knew we weren't due to go to Marcus' house before 6pm but I wanted to be ready, to have everything loaded in the car and to just spend the afternoon on my porch with a glass of lemonade feeling blessed.

Once the kids were up we started loading the car with the "important treasures" as Lily put it and then checked the small trailer we had borrowed was attached and ready to be loaded. Rigo came over slouching and moody but we all knew it was because he was going to miss us so we ignored him and just gave him stuff to put in the trailer.

The day passed so quickly and the kids got more and more excited with every hour. I overheard Lily tell Jason that he would be in charge of looking after the dog as she intended to use the swimming pool to train as a synchronized swimmer. It made me laugh and their excitement was contagious, even Rigo was happy once I told him he would have to come and cook for us at least four times a week or we would starve without him.

"I knew you would say that, seriously Sol, you need to learn to cook one day" he scolded.

At 6pm we all looked at each other and after a tearful and very long goodbye to Nana and the girls we jumped into the car and headed West.

After about forty-five minutes you could smell the sea air and the breeze kicked in. The sun was low in the sky but still warming the world and shining bright.

"Are we there yet Ma?" asked Lily, eyes wide and with still hands clenched in her lap.

"Almost baby, about five more minutes. Are you scared sweetie?" I asked, suddenly worried that this might not be so simple for the kids to understand.

"Yes Ma, I am a little scared. The house seems like it will be really big and I hope Marcus is as nice as you say he is. We will be well behaved Ma, we will look after the dog and we won't make any messes I promise" she spoke so quickly I could barely understand her.

"Make messes? Lily, please don't worry so much about this move. We are going to have a blast and Marcus will love having you guys there. Lily we will stay and enjoy ourselves and do what we normally do. It is only for a month and then we will find a newer and better place that will be ours forever and you can make as big of a mess as you want to" I tried to reassure her.

"I know Ma, you always make things okay and I know we will have fun, I guess I am just a bit nervous about meeting new people and having a new life" she looked at me wide-eyed.

"I understand that sweetie, and I will be with you all the time so don't worry about anything. I love you and Jason so much I will make sure we have loads of fun and that you are happy. You and J mean the world to me and more, I only want to make you both happy!" I told her brightly. She looked out at the sea and smiled, I knew she was excited and looking forward to a new adventure, she got that from me.

Rigo turned into the red brick drive and the house came into view, the children were silent and bug-eyed when they saw the beautiful house they would temporarily call home. Rigo parked up next to a shiny chopper with a dragon drawn onto its tank and whistled as his eyes drank it in.

"That is a sick bike, you know they only made three and each one has a customized dragon on it drawn by none other than Felix Constada!" He looked at Jason to make sure he was listening, "they say when the three bikes are united the dragons come to life and play in the sky above the riders!"

"Really? Dragons?! Is this true? Have you ever seen it?" asked Jason.

"I've never seen it myself but I would like to believe some magic still exists in the world Jay! What do you think of the house?" Rigo asked

"It's so big I will need a map! I am kind of scared to go in actually, I want to go back to Nana's" he whimpered.

"Don't be a baby Jason" Lily scolded, "Mama wouldn't bring us here if it was a bad place! You haven't even seen the pool wimp. Give it a chance!"

Rigo turned off the engine and then I realised I could hear my own heart beating, I felt glued to my seat and found myself just staring at the backseat at the children as if I was seeing them for the first time. My thoughts were all over the place but quickly interrupted by the sound of a door opening and a dog barking. My eyes stayed on the children as they saw Marcus for the first time as I wanted to get an honest insight to what they must be thinking. Jason slid down onto the floor while Lily sat up taller but otherwise made no move. I looked over at Marcus as he waved towards the car with one hand and held the dog back with the other. He was dressed casually in shorts and a navy blue t-shirt with a huge smile. Lily perked up a little and waved back timidly whilst Jason peeked his head up above the seat so he could assess his new charge.

I reassured myself with the memory of my conversation with Xavier and straightened myself and opened the car door. Rigo followed my lead and we both got out of the car and walked over towards Marcus.

“Hey Soleil, how are you doing? He asked as he extended his hand out to shake Rigo’s hand “How you doing bro” he said kindly.

"Hey Marcus, good to see you again." he replied.

"Are the little people in the car hiding from me or the dog?" he asked jokingly.

"Probably you as they have never been scarred of dogs before!" I said slightly shyly. I was searching his face for any negativity as I couldn't believe Marcus was still so relaxed about having his house invaded by complete strangers.

"Well you made it and this is what we agreed so let's get the stuff moved in and get you guys comfortable. Sylvia has been in today and briefed on you guys moving in so she made up three rooms since we didn't know if you want to share or each have your own space, you decide."

I had never been faced with such a question and had no idea how to respond. We would be happy crammed into one room or sleeping on the floor! I starred at Marcus with what must have been a dumb look and started walking back towards the car without answering. The men followed me and as we reached the car I could see Lily sitting up straighter and fidgeting with her hands that hadn't moved from her lap possibly the whole journey. I snapped out of whatever reverie that had gripped my brain and smiled at both the children.

"Marcus, I would like you to meet Lily and Jason, my children"

"Hello Lily, hello Jason, it is lovely to meet you. I hope you are not scared of the dog, he's loud but harmless!" he said but was met with silence and wide eyes.

Suddenly, Jason whispered from his half-hidden spot, "Have you seen the dragons?"

"The dragons?" Marcus asked bewildered

"Felix Constada's dragons, from the bike" offered Rigo smiling.

"Oh ya, those dragons! Not yet, we haven't had the three bikes together yet but one day we will and I hope the myth is true, I'd love to see dragons, wouldn't you?" he asked.

"As long as they were not hungry I guess it would be ok" replied Jason sensibly

We all laughed slightly nervously as we were not expecting dragons to feature in our first conversation; but it was a good ice breaker and I saw Lily relax slightly and Jason stood up in the back of the car to have a proper look around his new surroundings.

“Tell you what, before we get to the unpacking why don’t we go inside, I’ll show you around, and you can see what rooms you want and where everything is. That way we know where to put everything. I’ll show you the garage too in case you want to store some of your stuff there” Marcus said more to Lily than anyone else as she hadn’t made a sound yet.

“That sounds like a lovely idea Marcus, what do you think kids?” I asked with enthusiasm.

“Ma, can we see the pool first?! Please?!” Jason pleaded

“That is a perfect place to start” quipped Marcus.

Rigo helped Jason jump out of the car and looked at Lily and offered his back to her for a piggy back which she happily accepted. With the kids in tow Marcus led us around the side of the house and into the backyard where the pool was shimmering in the fading sun and beyond the cliff edge you could see the diamonds dancing on top of the sea.

“Lily! Come on lets go check it out!” Jason shouted as he ran towards the pool. Lily finally made a small sound as she jumped down from Rigo’s back and followed her brother.

I looked over at Marcus, who looked amazed to see children running around his backyard, "Thank you Marcus, for doing this, for giving us a chance and .."

"Lily, Jason, come on lets go inside so we can start unloading the car! I haven't got all night!" bellowed Rigo and the kids came running over.

"No worries Soleil, just make yourselves at home." He smiled and started walking off towards the house.

Lily ran right after him and as soon as she was close enough she tugged his shirt and said "Excuse me Sir, I wanted to say hello properly to you now. I was shy before and I was quiet, I wasn't being rude I think I was just nervous" Her words came out almost all at once but said with such relief she looked so little again. Marcus knelt down in front of her and looked her straight in the eyes.

"Let's start again then. Hi Lily, I am Marcus and I am very pleased to meet you. I just have one request.."

"Good evening Sir, I am Lily" she interrupted and did her best princess courtesy.

Marcus chuckled and bowed his head towards her. “One request Lily, please call me Marcus, I am still waiting for the Queen of England to give me a knighthood!”

“Have you met the Queen of England?!” she said in complete awe.

“Yes, very briefly when we did a big charity concert in London” he said making it sound so very casual.

“WOW” she whispered, “that is amazing... Marcus” then she ran back towards me and grabbed my hand. “Ma, he has met the Queen of England!”

We started off again towards the house and Jason confidently bounded along to the delight of the dog that looked happiest of us all.

Marcus took us inside and began his tour of the house. He started in the living room where my picture hung.

“Ma, look there is an angel in that picture!” Lily exclaimed. Marcus stopped dead in his tracks and turned to look at her. He was about to speak but stopped himself; a brief wave of sadness washed over his rugged features and disappeared as he led us through to another living room.

"This is the main TV room, you can close all the blinds and have popcorn and pretend you are at the movie theatre anytime you want!" he said with enthusiasm.

Jason looked at me then Rigo then Lily, "Why don't you just go to the real movie theatre" he asked innocently enough.

Marcus laughed "I'm not allowed in anymore; too many people take pictures and disturb me every minute. So one day I decided to make this room instead and save myself the hassle."

Marcus continued with his tour and showed us what part of the house he normally hosted his guests in. He had prepared three huge bedrooms for us each one was decorated with simplistic, practical furnishings and the colors were warm and bright. Each room was ensuite with one having a floor to ceiling window facing the ocean just above a huge Jacuzzi bathtub. Soft plush towels had been laid out, each set a different color and bath bombs and candles were all ready for use. The children stood in amazement then went off for a private huddle before coming back to inform us that they would rather share a room because otherwise it would be a little too scary for them. They chose the bedroom with the view over the sea and left the luxury bathtub and candles to me.

The kids decided to go explore more of the backyard and get to know Dani, the dog, better, while Rigo and I headed back to the car to start unloading. Marcus was on a phone call and waved at us that he would come help in a minute.

"Damn, Sol, I feel like we are in the twilight zone or something. This guy is so chilled about you guys moving in here and check out the size of the rooms! The kids are never going to want to leave! You better get this project done and make it good cuz you just raised their expectations through the roof!" Rigo said as we untied the tarp over the trailer.

"Yeah, thanks bro, no pressure then huh?! But ya, he is so chilled out, I feel like it's a blessing, you know maybe we are meant to be here for this time. I was worried about Lily there for a minute but she seems better now" I answered as I lifted off the tarp. It struck me how little we actually brought with us. We had left a few boxes with Nana but otherwise all of our world consisted of was three suitcases, four boxes, my computer and editing equipment and three boxes of toys and "treasures" as Lily liked to call them.

"This shouldn't take too long" I said happily "Always good to live on the light side I guess. The three suitcases are all we really need tonight as we packed them for a month's worth of living. Oh and of course my equipment needs to be brought in and set up. I saw a lovely desk in my new room so we'll just put it there. The rest of the stuff we can put in the garage so we don't bring in too much clutter, he seems a bit of a neat freak so I don't think boxes would suit his decorative tastes!"

Rigo lifted the crate with my equipment in it, "I'll take this in and set it up for you. You move the suitcases in and then once Marcus is done we'll put the rest in the garage."

I turned back to the trailer to unload the suitcases when Marcus came out of the front door looking slightly worried.

"Hey Soleil, sorry about that, that was Hugo our bassist" he explained.

"Not to worry, Rodrigo and I were just unloading. We were going to ask you to open the garage so we could put most of this in there, but no rush he's gone to.."

"Soliel, I'm not going on tour for at least another month, Hugo just sliced his finger to the bone trying to make sashimi for his wife's birthday dinner! He was at the hospital to have ten stiches and a blood transfusion!” he explained “The record label doesn’t know yet so we decided to tell them tomorrow and see what we can arrange.”

This was a huge and very unexpected surprise, we were supposed to just ‘housesit’ but now he didn’t really have a need for that. I started to panic slightly inside but kept my selfie smile plastered on.

“Oh wow, that is horrible for Hugo, did he sound ok?” I asked tentatively.

“Oh he’s fine, this is nothing, we have had some pretty crazy things happen over the years, ten stitches will be a breeze” he replied with slight nervousness in his voice.

We stood silent for a moment, almost frozen, the breeze in the trees making the only sound. I was suddenly worried that this plan was not going to work, he hadn’t agreed to us staying while he was home and now he was going to be stuck at home doing nothing except experiencing school summer holidays with strangers.

“You know Marcus” I started. “Soleil, I think..” he said at the same time.

“You go first” I said, “it’s your house.”

“You guys should still stay, please. I mean it was all sorted out before anything happened and the kids seem really excited. I won’t bother you guys and you can stay for a month, I really don’t mind.” He said as he examined the rope we had used to tie down the tarp.

“Marcus, I really didn’t expect this and I don’t want to burden you so unexpectedly. We can always go stay with Rigo, I mean we haven’t unpacked or anything and it’s no big deal, honestly. I don’t want to disrupt your daily life. I mean you didn’t expect this so maybe it was just meant to be..”

“No!” he interjected quickly looking straight into my eyes “No, it will be fine. We’ll figure it out. It will be nice to have some company and since technically I won’t have any work to do it doesn’t bother me at all if it doesn’t bother you I mean.”

I was so relieved to hear him say that, I had already started to calculate how many nights our savings would get us at a hotel as I knew going to Nana’s wasn’t really a viable option, we had nothing to fill a home with so I couldn’t get the house back and Xav already had tenents ready to move in. He seemed kind of relieved and he was smiling, I quickly decided to trust my fate and smiled back with a genuine grin this time. “Ok, sounds good, we’ll see how it goes I guess. If we drive you nuts we’ll go with no offence taken, promise!” I tried to weakly joke.

“Perfect!” Marcus said with a grin “Give me something to take in and then I’ll go open the garage. You will see that rocky mound open up in a minute, I call it the bat cave. I need to get my dragon inside too.”

He grabbed the biggest suitcase and started rolling it towards the front door, He seemed happy enough with this unexpected turn of events. I took a deep breath and thanked the stars we had a roof over us tonight, “please let this work, I just need one month” I whispered to no one in particular. I suddenly realised how twisted my stomach felt and stared up at the sky hoping for some sign all would be well. The crescent moon crept out from behind a feathery grey cloud and shone bright as the breeze carried the sweet scent of the sea to wash over me. I smiled, relaxed and took another deep breath, letting the air fill my lungs and replenish me with hope and positivity.

CHAPTER TWELVE

After a light supper and showers, the kids almost couldn't wait to go to bed. So I tucked them in, made sure they knew where I was and I went back to the kitchen as Marcus was making himself a cup of tea.

"Would you like some tea? Its camomile, helps me get to sleep" he asked with a grin.

"No thanks, sounds far too healthy for me, anyways, I sleep like a professional normally!" I realised how stupid that comment sounded so I just thanked him again for his hospitality and for letting us stay before heading off to my new room to work on my film. I had to stay focused, I had one month to get the project done and one month of free workspace so every minute I could I needed to work.

The next morning, the house was silent, Dani was outside and it looked like Marcus was still asleep so I decided to explore the kitchen and see if I could get breakfast going for the kids. When they joined me in the kitchen I had already buttered four pieces of slightly burnt toast and was looking in the fridge for some jam or something better to disguise the burnt taste. The kids were trying to reassure me burnt toast was their favourite and only when I agreed they could go swim straight after breakfast did they take the toast and sit down. Marcus strolled in shortly after and looked horrified at the toast and gave a very sympathetic look towards the kids.

“Good Morning! I thought I smelt burning. Dani wouldn’t even eat that Soleil, what happened?” he chuckled and walked to the blender on the counter.

“I can’t cook and toast is even a challenge but don’t worry I won’t make you any. I always admit when I am defeated and the kitchen always wins against me” I said with a sheepish grin.

“Wow, poor kids. Ya, no worries you leave breakfast to me, I have a special shake in the mornings anyways. Kids, leave the toast if you want, I think you will like my shake better. Just give me five minutes.” He set off opening cupboards and the fridge lining up all his ingredients.

“You are both in luck because Friday is my cheat day so I get to put in two scoops of Nutella! You guys like chocolate?”

"Chocolate milkshakes for breakfast?!" cheered Jason "This is going to be an awesome day Lil, I can feel it!"

Marcus put together loads of tasty ingredients, blitzed it up and poured out four big glasses and taking one for himself and gesturing to the kids to come grab one too. "There is one for you too Soleil, try it, it's not bad and sets you up for the day."

I was shocked, it was like waking up to kids and a stranger were perfectly normal for Marcus and he had taken making breakfast in his stride like it was the most normal thing in the world. He had headed out to the backyard to enjoy the morning sun and say hello to Dani.

"Can we go outside too Ma?" asked Lily

"Of course, but no swimming until after you've had your shakes ok. I'll go dig out your swimsuits"

"Ma, have your shake too, it would be rude not to right? They are delicious!" piped up Jason.

"I'll take mine to my room and get your stuff ready for the day; shall we go to the beach this afternoon?" I asked hopeful they would say yes.

"Of course, ma! It just down the cliff right?!"

"Yup. Excellent you guys explore but stay together today just till you get used to everything ok" I said cautiously.

I watched them timidly walk towards Dani and Marcus while they sipped on their shakes and thanked God that all was well so far. Marcus had woken up and seemed happy to have company and also seemed to take an interest in making us feel welcome and comfortable, like we had been friends forever.

The day passed wonderfully, the beach was virtually private and the water was calm and clear. Marcus had gone out after some lunch so we headed off with Dani and had a great swim and played on the sand. With rumbling bellies, we headed back up the steps towards the house and were met half way up by the smell of BBQ. I figured he must have a neighbour nearby and what a great evening to BBQ.

We reached the top of the cliff and I was amazed. It was Marcus at the BBQ and a table of bread and salad was set up next to him. I couldn't believe he was cooking for us! An international rock star, humbly grilling some chicken on the BBQ for some random woman and her kids who had invaded his house only the day before? This was a dream and I for one did not want to wake up!

"Hungry guys?" he asked with an easy smile

"Starving!" replied Jason eyeing up the grill and potato salad.

"Marcus, you really didn't need to...." I started.

"You kidding, me and Dani have to eat too, one more, one less my mom always used to say. Food is always better when it's shared, besides I didn't do much, just some shopping and turned on the grill. I hope you all like chicken!" he asked as he turned back to the grill.

I think I looked like I was in shock, as Lily pulled my arm and almost woke me up.

"Come on ma, don't be rude! Its BBQ, your favourite!" she reminded me as she pulled me towards the table.

We had an excellent dinner; over stuffed ourselves and all lounged in the beautiful seats around the pool. After relaxing a while I got up to clear away the table and Lily jumped up to help.

"Don't worry about that, I'll get to it later." Marcus advised.

“No way Marcus, after that it’s the least I can do! Besides, Nana always said that if you don’t cook it you have to clean it up. I think that is partially why she was always cooking, she never was a fan of cleaning! Anyway, thank you for dinner Marcus it was delicious!” I said as I turned towards the kitchen.

After washing up and dipping our feet in the pool, the kid’s yawns just wouldn’t stop. They both climbed in my lap and we had a cuddle. Then they got up, gave me a kiss and headed off to bed. As they were going inside Marcus came out, unexpectedly Jason threw his arms around him and gave him a huge hug.

“Thank you Marcus, you are so cool and dinner was awesome! I have had such a good day, thank you!” he let him go and walked into the house as Lily offered Marcus her hand.

“Thank you Marcus, I also had a wonderful day and dinner was really tasty. Thank you for cooking for us, especially Ma, besides Tio and Nana no one ever cooked for her. Good night!” as she scampered behind Jason into the house. I saw their bedroom light come on and two little excited shadows jumping around probably reliving the day. It made me smile and also distracted me from Marcus who was coming towards me with his cup of tea.

“Thanks Marcus, dinner was great. I can’t believe Jason hugged you, he is normally so shy.” I remarked.

“You’re a blessed woman Soleil, those kids are amazing and so pure and full of life! I have enjoyed seeing them enjoying the house and the pool and I think this month is going to be a lot of fun for all of us. Just promise me one thing” he asked.

“What? Ya sorry I just still can’t believe you’re so chilled out” I murmured.

“Promise me you will chill out, you look so stressed. You guys are welcome here, use it as you like and make the most of it. Leave the cooking to me please as burnt isn’t a flavour I enjoy too much and trust me, I think the kids are great so we’ll have loads of fun.” He said with a cheeky grin.

“I’m sorry Marcus, I guess it’s just the motherly instinct, I don’t want them to worry about anything and I don’t want to stress you out by being too troublesome. But if you are happy with this arrangement and if you take on the cooking I will do the cleaning and promise to get to work and enjoy this time with you guys. Just know how grateful I am and how happy I am that this is working out. We've been through a lot recently and you have really helped us out of a massive situation that would just be terrible for them. One day I'll pay you back, maybe not with money as you clearly don't need it. Maybe I'll get to capture your angel again for you." I said staring out over the sea and enjoying the silence.

After a few minutes, he said, "Hey, just relax and enjoy yourself. Do what you have to do and leave the fun and shenanigans to me. I'm sorry it is pain that has led you here, but know you are safe here. I am genuinely past my crazy and wild days so looking forward to some normal home stuff I guess. Me and Hope are the only ones in the band without a wife and kids you know. I think I might actually get it now when they talk about it." He stopped abruptly when I swung round to look at him in disbelief.

"Not that I see you guys like that but you know what I mean right?" he quickly replied sheepishly.

"Ya, I get it. Seems a win win for us all. Thanks Marcus, Goodnight." I flashed him my brightest smile and went inside to get a few hours of work in before bed as I suddenly felt defensive, I thought it was clear I was here as a guest nothing intimate was going to happen, I needed it to just be us three and our new start, new place, new life. I wasn't here looking to complete a rock star's life, and just be entertainment. I knew he didn't mean to offend me but I had to make it clear, this was an arrangement of choice for both sides.

CHAPTER THIRTEEN

Two weeks passed without major incident. Rodrigo and Nana had come over a handful of times and Nana developed a massive soft spot for Marcus; she was constantly trying to feed him and advise him that he needed to settle down and have some kids. He found it hilarious and genuinely appreciated the attention. International stardom had left him a keen observer of life but not arrogant and he seemed to enjoy helping them in the kitchen and easily joined in whenever those two ridiculed my cooking. He encouraged Rigo to take his van out and get started. He put him on to a few guys he knew that ran small festivals and would give him access to set up for the day for a small cut. Nana heard this and was suddenly interested.

"You do this Mijo, we will do this together. It is time to work, call them!" she slapped the back of his head gently but stern. I laughed and a red faced Rigo had to hide his grin.

The relaxed atmosphere was helping me finish up my work quicker than expected and the children loved that the hardest decision they had was swimming in the pool or the sea every day. Dani had taken to sleeping in their room almost as a guard dog and Marcus automatically made enough breakfast smoothie for the four of us every day. We all enjoyed every day and Marcus showed up with a pool volleyball set so they started a championship league that was invite only and very lively. They even got Nana in the pool one day to try it out.

Nana had come especially that day to help Marcus fix up an authentic Mexican diner for his bandmates and their families. He had asked my permission to invite them round as he didn't want to scare us off, but I was so shocked that he even asked I agreed within half a second. I had met the band before and I was looking forward to meeting their families and having more kids around to play with Lily and Jason. So after our morning swim and volleyball competition Marcus was handed a long list of ingredients and instructions from Nana and told the best place to buy the shrimp. He took the list and genuinely looked confused by some of what Nana had scribbled down. Lily started laughing and grabbed the list from him.

"Nana, he doesn't know what half of this is! I better come with you Marcus or you will never find Nana's stuff. Trust me if you disappoint Nana she'll give you food poisoning!" she finished off with a mocking laugh.

"You are right Lily, if you're happy to come out with me I would be grateful. I am more scared of what Hugo will say if I don't deliver this feast!" he said with a sparkle in his eye.

Suddenly realising that she was about to go out in public with a massive superstar dawned on Lily and she almost froze in her tracks. I knew exactly what she was thinking and could spy on the million and one scenarios she was playing over in her head.

"Will we be ok, if I come out with you Marcus? I don't want people to harass us or anything like that." She asked timidly.

"Tell you what Lily, I will put on my special blonde wig and you can wear my pink one, then no one will ever know it is us! Oh, and we'll take Ma's car since no respectable rock star would be seen in a station wagon!" he said with a smile.

"Hey, that baby has been amazing to me! Nothing wrong with vintage and comfort!" I retorted.

"Just kidding, Soleil, but ya we'll take your car and be back in a few hours. Let me go get the wigs

Lily, it will be fun!" he strode off to his rooms and Lily started jumping around and smiling.

"Be safe Lily, and don't forget to say hi to Guermo at the fish store. Tell him Nana said no rubbish today, only the best!" added Nana.

"Here you go Lily, see if that fits. Soleil the keys please and let's get going!" Marcus bellowed clearly excited to be shopping incognito in his long blonde locks and with company.

"Have fun guys, see you later!" I called out as I threw him the keys and waved off Lily. I went back to chopping onions for Nana with a smile on my face, happy that Lily was happy and back to being herself. She had been so quiet since Brody left, she always looked so worried.

"Soleil, mija, you done good. Look at Lily, she is happy, she trusts him and she is smiling again. I thought you were crazier than Rigo but you know what, maybe this arrangement was just what you all needed." Nana said from behind me.

"I'm glad you think so Nana, I miss you guys so much but this house has been amazing and it is such a great place for the kids. Marcus is like a big kid himself! Jason already tried to hussle me at pool yesterday and Lily is winning the volleyball league! He makes us food and just lives like a normal person Nana. No glamor or glitz, just a normal dude enjoying life." I gushed a little too eagerly for Nana's liking.

"Watch yourself Mija, guard your heart. Don't be too fooled by what you see and ignore what you don't see. In a few weeks this all ends and he will go back to being on the road and doing all those things they do, you will be homeless and still running a rat race. Please tell me you started looking for something, you only have two weeks left on this agreement, don't expect him to extend it. You stay independent Mija, no more wounds to clean and no more heartbreak for the children. Remember, the babies can't run next door this time" she said in her most authoritative voice.

"Don't be silly Nana, Marcus is a friend and someone who helped us out, I really appreciate that and am grateful. But I know how this life works too and I've been to see two houses in Long Beach by the sea already with two more visits planned next week. I can use the money from Xavier to put down a deposit and then hopefully the project I'm working on will be done and I'll get paid for that. So we all carry on according to plan." I told her with a firm nod of my head, almost like I was telling myself instead of her.

The air got heavy all of a sudden and Nana just kept watching me so I headed outside to start setting up the garden in anticipation of our guests and she started rummaging in the kitchen for her weapons for war on the groceries. I couldn't believe Lily had offered to go out with Marcus, she barely went out without me or Jason and she always took so long to get comfortable with new people. Jason came outside rubbing his eyes and looking super soft and cuddly.

"Where is Lily? I fell asleep Ma, the volleyball is getting harder!" he asked sleepily.

"She's gone to the store with Marcus baby, come here and have a cuddle with me" I persuaded with wide open arms.

Instead Jason stood still and opened his eyes wide.

"No way! Why does she always get to do the fun stuff! I want to go out with Marcus, Ma! How come she got to go?" he stamped his foot and pouted.

"Hey, J, you were asleep kid and Marcus needed help so Lily went, simple as that. Next time you can go with him ok? Now, stop being moody, Nana is in the kitchen and we are going to have a big party tonight so let's have a cuddle and then you go help Nana!" I replied with enthusiasm.

"Ok Ma, but next time I get to go right?" he asked as he buried his face in my neck.

"Yes, of course, baby, next time you can go out with Marcus. I guess I didn't realise how much you two like him." I said wistfully.

"He is awesome Ma, he is like an uncle now. He has so much fun and he doesn't care if we are loud like Dad used to. No, I like him Ma, I am glad he let us stay. I don't want to go back to the old house now."

"Well we will have to go somewhere in two weeks Jason, I am sure Marcus will always be our friend though. I'm glad you are happy. If you and Lily are happy then I am happy." I said through the shock of having the image of Brody pop back into my head. My back started itching, like the scars had come back to life and were prickly with anxiety.

"J, baby, scratch my back for me, like a bear cub please" I asked sweetly.

"No problem mama bear!" as he set to his task. "Ma, why does your back feel so lumpy now, did those bad marks not go away yet?" he asked sweetly with concern.

"No not yet gorgeous, but they will. Especially if you keep scratching!"

"I love you Mama Bear, I am so excited about the party tonight! I am going to go help Nana, she always needs me to taste everything" he said seriously and leapt off my lap.

A shiver went down my back and I found myself recalling good memories Brody and I had shared over the years. I smiled and shook my head, how stupid to hold on to those memories, look where it got us. Two weeks away from homelessness, far from the place we knew as home and nearly broke. I sighed and prayed the film would be a success and be enough to get us out of here. I still hadn't told Marcus I was even making the film as I didn't want him to think I moved in to enhance what I had already and I definitely didn't want him to know I was the film creator when they were showed the film by the record label. I closed my eyes firmly, looked up towards the sky and listened to the sea, after five deep breathes I felt ready to hit the ground running again. I was looking forward to tonight too, a bunch of aging rock stars and their families having a normal Friday night get together, sounds fun I thought. What could go wrong?!

It was 8pm and the party was well underway. Nana's menu was going down a storm and Marcus was a very able sous chef. I found him in the kitchen refilling a tray of mini enchiladas with Nana warming up more tortillas, both were laughing and looked to be in great spirits.

"Soleil, how's it going? Having fun? The boys are loving Nana's food, I have never seen all the kids eat so much without complaining. Nana, you could start a feed the kids of the stars program and make a fortune!" he laughed as he left the kitchen with his tray piled high.

"Hey Nana, how are you doing? You not too tired? Have you eaten?" I asked casually.

"Mija these people are so kind. They all want me to come cook for them every week!" she giggled, "Loca! If my mama could see this she would never believe it!" she looked over at me, "Mija you ok?"

"Ya Nana I am great. You are right these people are really kind and the kids are all having so much fun. It's great, really great. Hey Nana, where is Rigo? What time did he say he was coming with the girls?" I asked concerned.

"He said he would be here by 7:30 to help me out but he's always late Mija, besides Marcus is a good replacement so I can't complain. Why don't you call him and see how long he will be" she said over her shoulder as she took more guacamole out of the fridge.

"Ok, I'll go out front to call his cell. You sure you are good? You don't need my help?" I asked as I walked towards the door. I didn't even wait for her answer, I knew I was the last person in the world she would let touch her food!

I went out the front door to call him in peace, but just as I was dialling his car pulled in. His sisters were in the back and everyone looked like they had just seen a ghost as he glided up to park but didn't turn off the engine.

"Rigo, what happened? You all look like death! Did you have an accident? You ok?" I asked suddenly panicked.

"Soleil, I need to talk to you. It's bad." He said solemnly. The girls jumped out the back "You two go in and help Nana and have fun. Leave this to us, ok." They gave me a quick hug as they walked inside quickly, almost desperate to get out of the car and away from Rigo.

“Rodrigo, you are scarring me know, what the fuck is going on?!” I raged as I grabbed his shoulders through the window.

“It’s that piece of shit Sol, that son of a bitch. He’s dead. The police came to your old house and the new tenants told them to come to our house as they had no idea who he was or who you were. We were just leaving and the police knocked on the door asking for you. Apparently they found his car in a ditch and his body about a quarter of a mile away. He smashed up the car and then tried to walk away but he was so high according to the sample they ran. He ended up falling or slipping or something, smashed his head on a rock and bled out. This is what they told me but they do not have a positive identification on him so need you or me to come and do that.” he told me quite emotionlessly.

“Fuck off Rigo, fuck off. Not today, not now. No. He’d been in my head all day. What the fuck?” I mumbled confused and in shock.

“Sol, the fuckhead is gone for good now. I ain’t crying for him. Son of a bitch deserved an even worse death than that. I don’t want to see his ass but I’ll take you down so you can identify the waste of space and then they can throw his ass in a poor man's grave with the rest of the shit they clean up off the streets. Come on, pull your shit together and let's get this over with." He said sternly, like a father telling off his wayward daughter. I couldn't move, I couldn't process what he was saying.

The thing that was confusing me most was I wasn't upset, I was feeling almost relived and relaxed. If this was true then I would never be victim to his hands again nor would the kids and there was no chance of my heart betraying me and taking him back... ever.

"Let me tell the kids I have to go out and tell Nana we have to go out. I'll grab my purse and be back in five minutes." I rushed back into the house to the kitchen where I told Nana something came up and I had to go out with Rigo. The girls were with her so she didn't ask me much, she and I knew they would tell her what was going on. I looked outside and saw the kids in the pool with other kids, Marcus and Willow, the drummer, playing marco polo, so I told Nana to tell them I had to go out and to get them to bed sometime before sunrise. She agreed to stay the night as did the girls, so I headed back out the door in a mist and jumped in next to Rigo and without saying a word he pulled away.

The drive to the hospital was almost an hour, it was an hour of silence. I didn't trust myself to speak. I even thought that I would get there and it wouldn't be his body. Then what? He would be out there; he could find us again and then what? And if it was him, what do I tell the kids, do I even tell them? Surely it would be better if they knew but what if they got upset. I couldn't pinpoint my emotions, part of me wanted to cry but the bruised and battered face that looked back at me in the mirror that fateful night also haunted the back into my mind and reminded me that this was the best thing I could have asked for. If he was gone by his own hand and he had been high at the time then he obviously had no plan to fix himself up and come back to us, he had made the choice and that was that. I closed my eyes and tried to relax. Yes, he was gone by his own hands, no more pain, no more lies, no more excuses and no more him and the torment he brought to my heart.

Rigo parked up at the hospital and we jumped out. He put his arm around me and we walked into the reception where they gave us directions to the morgue. Just reading the word made me shutter and I started feeling cold. We got to the morgue reception and were met by a uniformed policeman who said a few greetings that didn't really make sense to me so I let Rigo do the talking. Rigo led me to a freezer room and there was one drawer pulled out with a sheet covered body lying still. I shrugged off Rigo's arm and raced to the body and ripped off the sheet.

It was him.

Head still bloodied and bruises all over but it was him. His naked frame gave away all his secrets, track marks up his arms and between his toes told the tale of his addiction. He looked pathetic, he looked trashed; he looked dead in every sense of the word. This thought caused my heart to soften, knowing with certainty he was gone gave me room to realise that Brody, my friend, was also gone.

I traced my finger along his cheek and mouth staring at his closed eyes and smiled. We had our time; we had our adventures and we had loved so purely. He had taught me how to survive and how to live a life when the whole world ignored you. He was my mom, my dad, my guide and teachers. I would walk away today with those memories and share those with the kids if they asked. I could tell them he died and comfort them because my heart was not aching; I was going to carry on and be strong, a survivor and give them everything now free from fear. I am not sure how long I stood by him and stroked his cheek just looking at his face and thinking of all those adventures we had had as kids.

“Goodbye Brody, thank you for the good times, the laughs and the love. Thank you for Lily and Jason, but thank you for going this way. Painless for us and a clean break with the past for me” I spoke these words as Rigo approached me.

“Don’t touch me Rigo, I am fine. Genuinely, I’m fine. It’s him isn’t it? 100%. Why did I ever think he would end up any other way. The chapter is done now Rigo, let’s go.” And I turned away from Brody and walked out the door.

“Ms Di Vittorio?” a voice called out. “Can I speak to you for a moment?”

I turned to find the uniformed policeman waiting with a bag and a notebook in his hands.

“Could I ask you some questions before you go? I am really sorry for your loss and...” he started.

“Don’t be sorry, I didn’t lose anything. Ya sure, what do you need me to do?” I asked.

“Well if you can positively identify him as Brody Maguire then I am free to release his articles to you. Will you be providing the funeral?" he asked totally oblivious to the history between me and the corpse.

"I will not provide him with anything officer, I'll let my tax money contribute to whatever funeral the state will provide. As for his articles, what did he have left with him?" I asked dryly.

He handed me the small brown bag "Not a lot I'm afraid, and nothing that looked very valuable. Should I assume that other then you there is no next of kin? No one I should notify?"

"Maybe tell a few dealers they lost a client but other than that no, No one." I answered solemnly.

I took the bag and it felt really light. I opened it and there was a phone and a small notebook. Right at the bottom something else caught my eye. It was red and I prayed it was not what I thought it was. I gingerly pulled it out and found myself holding the Love heart Jason had made that I had chucked out with him that night. It was symbolically broken in two pieces but otherwise still the same; how ironic, the love heart, forged by our child, taken in anger and with him when he died. I smiled through my tears. There was good in him, he did think of us, he didn't really want to be a junkie. He held on to this above all else, love, he always needed it but never had enough of it, just like the heroin, just like the crack, it was never enough.

"So Ms Di Vittorio, you can confirm it is him and you do not want to notify anyone else? Will you also take procession of his articles?" The officer asked me gently as he walked towards me.

"Yes, it is him. Our son made this heart, I would know it anywhere and it is the only thing I will take with me if that's ok. The only people to tell are his kids and I'll take care of that tomorrow. So ya, I think I am done here, you need me to sign something?" I asked.

"All we need is for you to sign this form and check the box that you authorise the state to bury him. Do you want notification of where he is buried?" he asked gingerly.

My head shot up quickly and startled him. "I didn't give a shit where he was when he was alive, why the fuck would I want to know where he is when he's dead?! What a stupid fucking question sir!" I answered angrily.

"Sol, chill out sis, it's all formalities. You know how it goes, just sign the paper and lets go home." Rigo interrupted.

"Mam, I know it isn't easy for you and I appreciate this is the last place you expected to be tonight, but the law says you are responsible for him as next of kin but the state will take care of things if you just sign the paperwork." the officer said calmly, trying not to agitate the situation .

"Fine, just give me whatever I need to sign to be free of this place and this headache. I said looking at the officer straight in the eyes, making sure he understood some of the pain I was in, but then I realised, this stranger had nothing to do with my situation, and he didn't ask to meet me tonight or pick up this piece of shit off the side of the road. I relented in my stare but unfortunately this opened up the avenue for two tears to slide down my cheeks. "I am sorry officer, thank you for your help." I took the papers and sat down with a pen and without reading the papers signed them and handed them back.

Rigo, sat next to me and gathered me up in his huge frame into his bear hug. It broke me, I couldn't stop the boulder from rolling away and releasing the flood. I sobbed like I would never stop; I couldn't see anything anymore, just tears and memories flashing before me. I was still so angry with Brody, still so hurt that he didn't choose me to live with, instead he sold his soul to his habit. He robbed me and beat me; he loved me and saved me. I felt like my insides were in a tangle. I didn't think I would ever stop crying. I wasn't sad in the least, just angry, disappointed and lost. The reality of my situation was staring me right in the face. I was a single mom of two, homeless, almost penniless, uneducated and living project to project in hope that one day the golden ticket would find its way to my wallet. Brody had saved me from the hell of the streets as youths but as adults we didn't work like I had hoped we would. It was all back down to me. It was time to stop crying, let the anger go and strive forward like I had promised myself I would do the night he whipped me like a stubborn ass. I had given my kids a safe place while I figured out this mess, I had let them be happy and enjoy themselves, thanks to Marcus they had a taste of what the good life could be and felt safe again. So now, it was time for me to find the next place for us, strike out bravely and stay determined and focused on what lie ahead. I had family, I had talent and I had love, more love then I could have ever hoped for. I was still strong, still able to stand and that is what Brody had left me no choice to do now. He gave me so much at one time and now he left me so little. My sobs settled down, I was exhausted. Rigo's shirt was a mess too. When I pulled away and looked at him he had been crying to, I could see the pain in his eyes but he tried to give me a smile.

"Soleil. You were due that; you've got it all out now. He is gone, you are free, let's go and let's make the most of whatever comes next. I have your back hermana, always. You and the kids are my life; I love you all so much. Come on, let's go." He said standing up and suddenly looking ten years older and wiser.

I looked up at him and smiled, he was right, I was free now, freer than ever before. I could go anywhere and do anything but all I wanted to do was get back to Marcus' house and see the kids. I still didn't know how I was going to tell them but I also knew there was no rush either. The police officer was still standing slightly away from us, just watching patiently. He looked like he would rather be somewhere else, maybe he had kids he wanted to see or knew someone who had ended up just like Brody did. I smiled at him and he looked a bit surprised.

"Officer, thank you for your help tonight. Can I give you my email address and ya, I've changed my mind, let me know where he ends up. Maybe one day we'll be able to do something for him but not today, tomorrow or anytime soon. I just think maybe his kids should be able to know where their daddy ended up, they definitely need to know one day how he ended up there, right?" I spoke to him as I made my way over to him standing with the paperwork still in his hands.

"No problem ma'am, just write it here for me. Ma'am, if you don't mind me saying, I am sorry for your loss but hope you see what you have gained. A man should never put his hands on a woman like that, he scarred you ma'am, let that be the last time you let anyone do that to you" he said with his eyes brimming with tears. "My mama suffered her whole life with my daddy, she deserved better, I deserved better, and that's why my kids get nothing but better."

He handed me the pen and I wrote down my details and looked up into his eyes, they had soul, they had understanding and compassion in abundance. I smiled again, warmed that goodness was still all around me. Good people had always come my way, Brody for a time was exactly what I needed, but now he was gone and new people were welcome to come back into my life. Unexpectedly, I threw my arms around the officer and gave him a huge hug; at first he stiffened up but then he relaxed and hugged me back.

"You are the nicest officer I ever met. Thank you. Thank you for your help and advice. I'll do the best I can not just for me but for the kids too." I pulled away and wiped away the last of the tears I would shed for Brody. "Thank you again, I'll wait to hear from you. I'm ready Rigo, time to go see what's next for us right?" I asked him wistfully.

"Sure Sol, lets go find out what's next for us." He threw his arm around my shoulders and shook hands with the officer, then we turned and made our way back to the car.

CHAPTER FOURTEEN MARCUS

"Marcus, bro, tonight was rad, thanks man." Hugo leaned in for a hug like he always did, "No problem dude, glad you and the family enjoyed it" I replied hoping he'd let go sooner rather than later. After a few drinks Hugo always got a little emotional and I really wanted him to get in the car before he tried to explain how much love he had for me for the hundredth time. Luckily his wife knew him too and shouted from the car to hurry up because the kids were exhausted from all the swimming. Hugo made his way, a little unsteady towards her singing an old Everly Brothers song loudly and totally out of tune. I stood next to Willow, all six foot five of him and we laughed. Hugo always had a good time, no matter what; he was the most positive person that lived on planet Earth.

"Marcus, tonight was awesome. Please convince Nana to come cook at my house otherwise I swear I going to starve. Millie has gone vegan and I swear there is nothing to eat in our house... ever! How's a man like me supposed to survive on tofu bro?!" He looked serious as he gestured to his broad six-foot plus frame, but then cracked his warm sincere smile and put his impressive arm around my shoulder. “Seriously bro, it was really cool tonight. It’s a shame that Soliel had to leave, she seemed real chill. I guess going by the people, even the little people, she brought into this house she must be something pretty special, huh?” he looked down at me and raised his bushy eyebrows, his knowing eyes twinkling mischievously.

I was lost for words only because so many wanted to come out at once. There was no way, in this brief moment, I could say anything that would even remotely convey all that had been running through my mind since Soleil showed up here with her crazy plan to move in. When I opened the door I could not believe she walked back into my life. I knew exactly who she was when I saw her face. That face, the one that was so lived, so dynamic, soulful and stunning. She had no idea what an impact she had that night at the concert on my heart; the picture she produced was a miracle especially as I had been missing mom so much. She had always loved my music good or bad and jamming with her was what lifted me to write more and speak my truth to the world and let each person feel what I had to say the way they needed to feel it and work it through their web of life. I can still close my eyes and go back to the moment Soleil must have taken the picture, I know mom was there, I felt better that day and now that picture always sets me back to what is real and important. That picture and Soleil's face merged and when she appeared again it was no surprise I agreed to let her and her kids move in, but I didn't want to scare her so I pretended not recognize her straight away. The kids, man the kids! It is so awesome to have little people running around, full of wonder and life. Always ready to test their limits and challenge you on yours. I really felt something for them already and I am sure it showed tonight, everyone didn't really need words from me for everything.

"So that's how it is bro. Ya, that's cool." Willow's voice broke the silent and gentle staring contest we must have been having, smiled wider and nodded. "See you real soon brother, we got work to do! Yee-ha boys, its back to the road for us!" he turned back to look at me, "Love you, M" turned on his favourite cowboy boots and headed towards his car. I noticed Nana had been generous with leftovers for him to take home. I smiled; Willow had been my buddy way back in the 80's. We'd journeyed together and always kept each other in check when fame and life took us away from ourselves and why we do what we do.

"Man, Marcus, we need to do this more often." Hope showed up behind me and clapped me on the back, "Being single at these things is the best. I get fed by a grandma all night and run around like one of the kids. Awesome jam tonight, honestly, best we've had in a long time. What happened to Soleil? I was speaking to her earlier in the kitchen, she seems cool."

I turned round and smiled at our youngest member. Hope is what Hope does. When he joined us he already knew all our most famous tracks. This was our second album together and he was flowing, doing his own thing and jamming. I loved having him in the band and he brought so much to the brotherhood because he had new ideas and was fresh, he brought a spark into the room that ignited everyone.

"I'm not too sure, Nana said something about having a problem at her old house, but I'm not sure." I answered suddenly feeling slightly perturbed that she had left and not been back; it was past midnight.

"Ah, hope it isn't anything too serious. Tell her I said bye and hope we see her again soon. Ooo tell Nana she is amazing, I am good for a week here brother, seriously I ate so much goodness tonight."

He stepped off the porch towards his taxi. Bachelor life, right… watch your buddies leave with kids, smiles, love and comfort while you leave with a stranger in the back of a car you don't recognise. Another part of your life where you sit alone and learn to enjoy it. Maybe you'll be a bit nuts and tell him to take you to a club, you get fucked in every way possible or you go home grab your board and go for a surf; there was no routine, but it was old. I prayed for better for Hope and realised, I kind of wanted Soleil to see them all soon. She hadn't come here by accident, but what it took for her to come at all, now that is what I needed a little bit of now. She had risked it all, maybe now it was my turn to at least ask her if I could get to know her better. Just be able to spend time with her that is consensual and relaxed would be all I would ask her to give more of. I could give her back so much; my spirit had been reawakened and wanted to try to give her so much back, but I was scared. I knew how to ride a fling, I could even long it out for a year or so, but she was different. She was someone I wanted to take time with. I wanted to really find out everything I could about her, she was a mystery to me; a complete enigma, but then sometimes it felt like I had known her my whole life.

When I walked back in the house the same usual silence was already broken and it sounded like a lullaby being sung. Someone was snoring down the hallway towards the kids room, music was still playing in the garden, Rigo's sisters were chatting loudly from their room and Dani was snoring on his bed in the kitchen. This felt really good, it filled me with energy and happiness all at once, I felt excited about tomorrow and hopeful.

There was no way I could get to sleep now and Soleil was still out so I went to the wet room changed into my wetsuit and grabbed my board. The sea was calling and I was definitely up for answering! The night was beautiful and the full moon lighted up the path to the beach and made the waves shimmer and shine. I could already see the sea was calm so I grabbed a paddle out of the beach hut and decided paddle boarding would be a better idea. The sea welcomed me and enveloped me into her chilly embrace. Immediately my whole body relaxed and pulled myself up on the board and stood up. I started paddling towards the rocky outcrop about a quarter mile off the shore with a beautiful light breeze at my back. I must have been paddling for about an hour when I saw a figure making their way down towards the beach, a shimmering vision in a white flowing dress that billowed all around it like a cape. I couldn't tell if it was a real person or if I was seeing something from the spirit world. The figure moved silently and quickly towards the shore; it looked like Soleil but she moved more mysteriously. I had never seen Soleil in a dress either so now I was actually convinced a ghost was heading straight out to sea. The ethereal figure dove out into the sea and reappeared to just float on top of the water. It didn't swim or move or make any noise at all. All the hairs were standing up on my neck and as bizarre as this apparition was there was something oddly familiar about its movement and tranquillity now. I started paddling closer as quietly as I could, I didn't want to disturb the enigmatic creature but I had to see what it was, I had to know what had brought it here. As I approached I could hear faint singing, not great singing but singing none the less. It was a song I knew, a song I had written in fact! The voice carried the words towards me "I got dosed by you..." The creature was singing the words to one of my most haunting songs, a song about a beautiful being that blessed the lives of all those it met. Drawing closer I couldn't believe my eyes, the creature was Soleil! She was so serene, her white dress flowing all around her like angel's wings, her voice drifting across the water like a prayer. Her eyes were closed, her long flowing locks were tied up loosely in a bun, I panicked as I thought she was in some sort of danger, why was she floating out here fully clothed and what happened to her?! I paddled right up to her, I needed to know what was going on, her behaviour was bizarre and worrying. I moved the board to within inches of her and her eyes flew open in surprise. Our eyes locked and she whispered "Hey Marcus, I thought you'd gone to bed.." I couldn't speak, she was so tranquil, she drew her head out of the water and started treading water calmly, like us meeting out here in the sea was the most normal thing in the world.

"Soleil, are you ok?" I suddenly had a million things I wanted to say to her.

"I'm great Marcus, I am sorry I had to leave like that, something came up. Are you paddling to shore?" she asked still totally calm and docile.

"Ya, sure, I guess.." I answered, impatient for answers and getting nothing but absolutely stumped by why she was out here floating in the sea.

"Cool, steady your board, I didn't realise how far out I came." She smiled as she pulled herself onto the top of my board and steadied herself with her back to me. "Is that ok for you?" she asked readjusting her sheath of white cotton that clung to her naked frame and dropped dangerously low down her back, only hinting at what gorgeous curves lie further south.

I had no words, nothing at all. Looking at her back all I could see was a raw crisscross of scars, they were not old, they were not new but they were definitely recent. Tears came to my eyes in a mixture of shock and anger. Who would do this, why did someone do this to her! This angel had been whipped like a horse and she must have suffered something nightmarish.

"Ya, I'm good. Are you ok? Are you cold?" were the only lame words I could get out as I didn't want her to hear how upset I was. Come on man, get a grip, calm down, I had no idea how we had ended up in this situation and how tonight would end but I wanted to be there for her, to help her if she would let me. She looked back at me and smiled her easy smile.

"I'm alright Marcus thanks, what are you doing out here anyways, I thought crazy sea person was a label I wore alone." My eyes drifted towards her back unintentionally and she realised I had seen her scars erasing her smile; she defiantly turned back around and squared her shoulders up looking straight ahead and saying nothing. I wanted to hold her, gather her up in my arms and just hold her. Why would someone damage her like this, why had this been her reality when she shone light over everything she touched?

I paddled us back up to the shore in silence and she jumped off and reached out to pull the front of the board up on to the beach. Checking I was docked first, she turned away and walked towards a small pile on the sand. I jumped off my board and secured it on the beach. It was a really warm evening so I unzipped my wetsuit and pulled the top half down. Soleil turned around and gasped as she saw my bare torso which immediately made me feel embarrassed as I didn't want her to get the wrong impression. I went to put the sleeves back on whilst I stumbled over my words.

"I am sorry Soleil, it's just really warm, I'm sorry I didn't mean to startle you." I was making a mess over getting the sleeves back on, I felt like a naughty boy caught with his hands down his pants!

"Marcus, don't be silly, I'm just being stupid. The whole world has seen your chest, I'm surprised you even wear a full wetsuit!" she smiled slightly nervously.

She stood up silently with something in her hands and turned towards me. Every hair on my body stood up on end. She was standing in front of me with her wet white dress betraying her beautiful shape and emphasising every amazing curve and contour of her body. I couldn't move, air was not going in, this marvel standing before me truly had me in a trance; I didn't know where to look and I am sure I was staring far too long. My eyes wound up her frame to her beautifully arched neck and noticed she was staring out to sea. She hadn't realised how exposed she was as she stood up tall with drops of water slowly tumbling down her face and back, like a fairy was sprinkling her with pixie dust, enhancing her beauty and amazing attractiveness. I suddenly felt perverse, as if I was spying on her in a very private moment. She wasn't speaking and it looked like tears were mixed in with the sea water rolling down her face and off her once glorious neck that had been scolded by strikes from the forge of fire and anger; concern was suddenly overriding my moment of adoration.

"Soleil?" I called her softly; I was growing worried now; I didn't know what to do with this beautiful creature. She was like an injured bird, still but so telling, I worried she would take flight and leave me on the beach. I wanted her to unleash the torrents of her mind. I wanted to know what had happened to her, not just tonight but before, why had she suffered so badly, why had she not been treasured and cared for. She didn't move when I called her name, she only closed her eyes and let the accumulated tears roll down her cheeks.

"Soleil? Please.. what happened? Your back..." I pleaded gently and stopped as she turned towards me and clutched the small objects in her hands. I just starred at her at a complete loss, I wanted to hold her and comfort her but I had never even shaken her hand before and I didn't want her to feel uncomfortable but with all the emotions and conflicting instincts fighting inside me I took a step towards her. She met my eyes and stood clearly in front of me. Her dress still clung to her and the short train behind her looked like it was keeping her rooted to the spot where she stood. She held me by my eyes for an eternity, tears continued to roll down her face yet she started to smile, slowly and only from the corners of her gorgeous lips.

"Soleil? Please..." I was pleading now, I didn't know what to do, I didn't know what was going through her mind. I went to take another step towards her and stopped. She raised her hand indicating to me to stay still.

"Marcus, I don't know what is happening. I feel strange, I feel free, I feel sad... but I feel.. I feel again.." she whispered still holding my stare.

"What can I do? Please let me help you." I took a step towards her as a look of surprise crossed her face.

"Help me? You have done so much already for me Marcus, I could never repay what you have done for me. Never. I am so grateful.." she said so softly I could barely hear her.

"Soleil, I don't mean help like that. You and the kids have been a blessing to my house, for the first time it is a home and that is because of you. But please let me help you now, what has happened, where did you go?"

She shook her head and rubbed the tears out of her eyes. She took two deep breaths and pulled her shoulders back. Suddenly she realised how exposed she was and how little discretion her dress afforded her. She became embarrassed and quickly covered her breasts and pelvis with her hands. She looked at me embarrassed and panicked.

"Oh my goodness! Marcus I am so sorry, I didn't realise.. I didn't mean ..." she was looking around for something to cover herself with.

Practicality won over at this point and bringing comfort to her became my priority, she clearly was not herself.

"Come. Let's go up to the beach hut and get some towels for you okay? I set off towards my beach hut that was full of towels, toys and everything I could never be bothered to bring back up to the house. "Come on, it's okay, I am sure I have towels and clothes up there."

I turned to walk up the moonlit path to the hut, when I turned around to make sure she was coming I was struck again by how ethereal and majestic she looked. It was like I had been sent my own little mermaid, lost, lonely, lovely and lustful all at the same time. She hadn't moved from where she stood though, she was also no longer shy or embarrassed about her unintentional state of undress either. She looked directly into my eyes and held me frozen to the spot.

CHAPTER FIFTEEN

"I only wore this dress once before Marcus... it was for a beach party." I said breaking away from Marcus' longing and uncomfortable stare straight into my eyes and looking down at my now see-through dress while holding it up out of the sand. Aware I had completely revealed the secrets of my body to him I fell unabashed, I wanted him to hear the truth and see I would not hide anything, and maybe he wouldn't be ready for everything.

"It was a beautiful summer that year and we were celebrating our friend's launch of their first studio album. We had all snuck away from the boring corporate launch as quickly as we could and got down to our favourite beach. We set up a fire and drinks and were just having a jam and enjoying a beautiful summer's evening. I was there with Brody, he is the children's father and also the man who gave me these scars. I guess in that sense I'll never forget him but that night was one I had treasured before tonight.

You see Brody and I met in elementary school. We were always the loners in the class, a little dirty, neglected, always hungry but always surrounded by music. We didn't have a lunch but we had a Walkman stitched together with scotch tape and rubber bands! We would listen to whatever we could get our hands on and one day the janitor George gave us his portable radio so that we could listen to classical music, jazz, rock... anything! George probably saved our lives. He used to give us whatever he found around the school like pencils, books, food and clothes. George gave me my first camera in fact, that is what truly set me free. Home really sucked for both of us. Brody lived with his Grandad who became a crack addict after his Grandma left them and he never knew his parents or why he ended up living with his dad's parents. My home was a nightmare. My dad left us and my mom was an alcoholic and worked as a prostitute so I was more a by-product of work then her child as my dad was never convinced to stick around and make a life with a whore. I never knew who or what would be at home so I never went home. I used to sneak in Brody's window once his grandad passed out and sleep there most days. We looked after each other, we had each other's back. We knew we would have to rely on each other to survive and we also knew we wanted better. We always said we would not end up like our guardians and we would never look back. We made the whole of LA our playground and by the time we went to high school we pretty much lived by our own means. We dropped out of school at sixteen and hit the road. We didn't have much but we used what we had to buy a decent camera and started following bands around LA and whenever we could, scam our way onto their tour buses or get some work as a runner or a roadie. We loved our life; we were as comfortable sleeping in a bed as we were under the stars. My pictures started to make us enough money that we could get a small RV of our own and we found a remote beach that we used to park up by and set up home. Things were good, against the odds we had found a home and safety and love."

I paused, I knew I was rambling but Marcus had yet to say a word, I wondered if he was even standing there. When I looked up at him his face was warm and he had a protective look on his face. I held his eyes and continued my story.

"So the night I was talking about... ya it was such a beautiful night, the moon was full, like tonight, and the sea was calm. The sand was still warm from the heat of the day and the company was awesome. Brody kept staring at me from afar but he was quiet, smiling but quiet. Once the music and fire died down, he grabbed my hand

and asked me to go for a walk with him towards the rocks further down the beach. He had made a little fire for us and had a blanket spread out. He told me that tonight, in this dress, I was gorgeous, that I looked like a bride and it was like our wedding night. He promised me that every day he would work hard to make me happy and keep me safe. He promised to love me forever and never hurt me. He thanked me for saving him and I thanked him for saving me right back. It was perfect, I actually thought we would make it and have a good life together. From that day forward we lived as man and wife, took on the world and immersed ourselves in a world of music, love, laughter and the beach."

"So what has happened now Soleil?" Marcus asked with enquiring eyes.

Instinctively I reached for my hair, remembering that I had tied it up less than an hour ago and it probably looked terrible. That combined with my choice of clothing and weird behavior must be a sight to behold. I felt a pull towards Marcus at that moment I couldn't explain. Here I was at probably my most vulnerable moment and he, he who had already given me so much was standing firm in front of me. He wasn't running or writing me off as a lunatic. I felt safe again, I felt like telling him every story I could remember from before. I wanted him to know me as intimately as Brody had and still accept me in the same way he had welcomed us into his home.

I took a step towards him, openly displaying all that I was. The dress did little to hide my nudity and the hair did little to hide my scars. I wanted him to see me up close, see what I was made of and how life had battered me but I was still standing, still strong. He didn't back away, just stared at me with his questions burning into my eyes. I stood still again, met his gaze and continued with my story.

"We did well enough for ourselves, we had some hard times but who didn't? Lily came along nine months after the most glorious trip I ever had to Mexico and Jason followed three years later. The kids brought us closer even still but Brody was always worried he would fail. Always worried that he would fall back into drugs or just be a waste like his grandad had been. We moved into a lovely little house next door to Nana and Brody worked when and wherever he could to support us. I carried on with my photographs and video editing which meant I could stay at home with the kids. Life was good. Life was really kind.

Then he went back into heroin. The flowers came a feasting and heroin came and snatched him away from me. He ended up loving that shit more than us. I tried to cover for him all the time. I was the only one blinded by love. He would have days where he just couldn't get up, other days he had no gear and would be violent. He became erratic, nonsensical and on that last night we were together, a demon.

Tears welled up in my eyes but I was not going to stop my truth being told. I needed to unburden myself, to try and process what had happened that night and tonight.

"The last time I saw him he was so fucked up. He was so violent and nearly killed me. Rigo literally saved my life. He was choking me and I had passed out. If Rigo hadn't come in I would definitely be dead and god knows what would have happened to the kids. I fought as hard as I could, I tried to defend myself but he got hold of Jason's school belt and that is what did most of the damage that night and has left me with these reminders. He left that night for good, I decided then and there he was no longer a part of us and told him to go and never come back unless he wanted me to allow Rigo and his boys to kill him. He did as he was told, gathered as much as he could get his hands on and was escorted to the nearest hole he could find by Rigo. So that was it. My paradise and dream had died because something else had become more important to him. The one person I thought I couldn't even breathe without was gone. Gone by his hands and my words."

"I don't know what to say Soleil. That is heart-breaking, you must be such a brave woman, you must be something amazing." Marcus said with emotion. Silent tears started to roll down my cheeks.

"Maybe, or maybe I am the dumbest woman you ever met. But like I said tonight everything has changed. The person who did this died tonight. That's where I was, Brody died tonight in a car crash, actually no he died because he was high and when he got out of the car he smashed his head and bled to death. They didn't know who he was but traced the car back to my old house and spoke to Rigo."

"He's dead? The kid's dad is dead? Was it the same guy who pulled you away the first time we met? Was he doing this to you even back then?" Marcus asked almost angry.

"When we met? What?" I was bewildered.

"When I met you, you gave me the photo that is hanging in the house now, remember? We were talking when out of the blue this guy came up to you and basically dragged you away from our chat throwing daggers my way the whole time!" he recalled "Do you not remember that Soleil? Do you not remember meeting me all that time ago?" he asked almost mournfully.

"I remember ever single word of that conversation Marcus; I remember the look on your face when you saw that photo. It was like my work had magic powers all of a sudden and your face was so grateful yet confused. I don't remember Brody pulling me away but he probably did, we were very protective over each other up until Lily was born." I could see the relief in his eyes that he wasn't the only one who remembered how meaningful that first meeting had been between us.

I let the silence sit between us for a few minutes, neither of us knew what to say because we had so much to say and didn't want to risk saying the wrong thing. We could feel the intensity in the air, we could feel the questions burning our hearts.

I reached up to my hair again.

"You know it's weird, lately these scars on my back have been so itchy. Lily has been amazing putting cream on them but I hate to ask her to do it too often, I feel like it is just cruel as whatever Brody was he was her father too. But lately they have been burning, like they knew he was close to the end. Maybe I should have looked for him, but I guess the burn reminded me of the pain I felt the last night and I never want to feel that again, Marcus. He broke me. Broke every ounce of dignity I had, I stood strong afterwards but felt so hollow. I guess as well I just want tonight to be like a metamorphosis. Tonight, the butterfly will emerge. I am free of the one who tormented my mind, body and soul. My children are free from him and our life cannot be blighted anymore by anyone. But we have no one else either, just Nana and her family... nana... when I saw her curled up with Jason inside tonight I realised she loves those kids like her own. I also realised something else Marcus. Something about you.."

I walked towards him and put out my hand, he took it cautiously. It was warm and I could feel his heartbeat, so strong, so much passion existed in him. His hand felt safe, caring and comforting. I looked at our hands and decided for a fresh start the truth had to be told.

"Marcus you have been a part of my life since the first concert I ever saw. Your lyrics always resonated with me and I used to pretend that every song you wrote you wrote just for me. When an album would come out I would listen and almost take ownership of the song after one listen. I took your messages with me wherever I went. I guess I felt like I knew you, that is why I never thought my crazy request was crazy, I knew you would at least consider letting us stay. I dunno, it just felt certain from the minute I thought of it and when Rigo randomly told me he had been to your house I knew it was written and I had to try my luck, Your songs never let me down and so far Marcus, neither has the man. You are amazing, your heart is enormous and the way you have just accepted all of us into your life, even Nana and Rigo, it's crazy. I mean Nana is totally at home sleeping in your house, cooking in your kitchen, telling you off and even trusting you to go grocery shopping for her. I can't believe how you have just accepted everything with a smile and been so chilled out about everything. I've told you before Marcus, and I can never say it enough; thank you; thank you for giving words to my growing pains, thank you for coming through your own troubles to keep the band together and growing into such a source of happiness and inspiration. The night I met you properly, your reaction inspired me to work harder on my talents. I thought if I could touch you the way you touched me with just a photo then it was a talent I needed to work hard on and enjoy; and I did. When life darkened with Brody the children and my work was all I had, I could put on music and disappear into whatever world I had on a screen in front of me."

I felt entirely unburdened, I felt like I had just shared a big secret with my best friend. I looked up from our hands to his face. I was shocked, there were signs that tears had journeyed down his face. I squeezed his hand and held his eyes, his gorgeous brown eyes, so full of warmth and shine.

"Marcus, I didn't mean to upset you, I never wanted that, I am so sorry..."

"Shh, don't apologise please." He pulled his hand from mine and wiped at his eyes. "I am just stunned, this is so surreal. You are here, not just here but really here. You think that much of me and my works, my life? I am shocked Soleil, really. You are an incredible creature and I am speechless. I have so much I want to say to you, but I can't. I am so scared of getting it all wrong and watching you disappear. I feel like I am in a dream and I don't even want to move for fear I will wake up and you... beautiful, ethereal you will be gone...Soleiel, you truly carry the light of the sun with you..."

I took his hand up again and turned up towards the beach hut. I gently tugged his arm to make sure he would come with me.

"Your face speaks a thousand words Marcus. Come; let's go see what you have in the hut to drink. I'll give you some time to get your thoughts together while we change. This is all so intense Marcus, tonight has been one like no other for me and I really don't know what tomorrow holds for me but right this minute I am happy and grateful it is your hand I am holding. I know with you tonight under the moonlight, dark clouds have been banished and respect has been restored. Come."

I led us up to the beach hut and Marcus took out some hoodies and shorts, told me to take whatever I wanted and I headed to the bathroom to change and have a shower. When I came out Marcus was sitting on the porch staring out onto the moonlit water. He had changed into an emerald green hoodie and black shorts that were identical to the ones I had chosen. He looked so strong from where I stood, he looked so assured and composed. If tonight was a shock to my system I could only imagine how confused he must be, I genuinely hadn't given any thought to tomorrow yet, I didn't know what I would tell the kids, I didn't know what other formalities would contact me or if Brody would somehow come back to life and haunt us. Pushing all the things I didn't know to one side, there was one thing I knew for sure. I didn't want to leave this place. I felt like I belonged here and I felt safe. Floating out in the water had taken me to my imaginary magical water world I always retreated to when life confused me. He hadn't panicked or pushed me, he merely accepted the situation and guided me back to safe shores, warmth and hope. I walked out onto the porch; he stood up and looked at me and smiled.

"Wow those shorts look great on you.." he laughed with genuine joy and his face lit up like a star. "You should keep them, you genuinely rock them."

"They don't look too bad on you either.." I replied with a chuckle.

"Come sit down, I only had a few beers in the fridge, is that okay? Do you even drink? I don't think I have seen you have drink." He asked suddenly nervous as if I would be offended by his offer of alcohol. Suddenly his smile faded and concern furrowed his brow. He turned to me with the most serious look on his face I had ever seen.

"Soleil, I know nothing of you, I know so little. I don't know where you have been, I don't know your favorite color, your favorite food...nothing" he looked down and took a deep breath before looking back up and asking "Soleil, can we change that? I know tonight has been horrible for you and I hope you don't think I am trying to take advantage... it's just seeing you so peaceful, floating in the sea and then finding out you had just identified your dead ex-partner, a man who terrorised you at the end...what can I say Soleil, I feel like I want to protect you, you and the kids. I want to hold you close and make your scars disappear..." he stopped suddenly. He had just vocalised something he wasn't prepared to say and perhaps even feel. He looked back towards the sea, I hadn't replied and I could feel his sudden worry.

"Marcus" I whispered slowly, "Marcus, look at me, please"

He turned back towards me and reached out for my hand again, I moved close to take it up.

"Marcus, tonight has been so emotional for me, I don't know what is real anymore, I am exhausted and so alive all at the same time. I feel so much for you but what, I don't know, I also know for certain that I don't want to leave in two weeks. I really don't... do you think we could stay a little longer with you?"

His face erupted into pure joy, his smiled reached both sides of his face. He pulled me in by my hand, straight into his chest and grabbed me into a huge hug. He said nothing, just held me close and let me melt into him. This hug was magical, the one you experience right before your whole life changes, the one that fills you with warmth and sincere care for the other person. It was a needed hug, we both had run out of words as everything was so highly emotionally charged. A hug was basic, primal and just what I needed so I hugged him back as hard as I could. He held me for ages, I could hear his heart, hear him breathing and at one point I thought I heard a sob get caught somewhere inside of him. I stayed wrapped in his arms for what felt like a year then I realised the moon had gone, the sky was lightening up. I pulled away slightly, our faces were only inches away.

"Does that mean yes?" I asked with a grin.

"Absolutely! But this time I have a few requests myself. I promise, I will not rush you to recover from tonight nor will I push you for answers about your feelings. But can I get to know you better, can I ask you questions, can we spend time together and explore the fate that has put us together in this place. I care so very much for you already Soleil, I care for your kids, for Nana, even Rigo! I won't push you to stay but please take me into your often silent world Soleil, let me know your thoughts and hear your heart speak. I want to carry on this journey with you Soleil, wherever it takes us, I want to experience life with you and the kids, even if in the end we realise we are only destined to be best friends. More than anything I just want to know you all and pray you all let me in and except my truths. My home and wealth is all made off of love, people I never met have paid for it, enriched me, enriched my life and my whole family. But now I have all these things but no one to share a single thought with, a single fear with. You chose to come to me, and I am choosing to come right back to you."

I fell against him again and hugged him as hard as I could. I closed my eyes and felt peace. Brody's dead face flashed in front of me and I held that image there. I held it as long as I could and when it melted into the face of my friend Brody, the Brody from school, the Brody from all the times he would be waiting at his window for me... my soulmate from the magical, impregnating waters of Mexico and I decided that was the image I would take forward with me. I would always see his smile in Lily's cheeks and his soulful longing in Jason's eyes but tonight whatever we had was gone, we would never speak another word, he would never get clean and come back to restore our family. He had truly left me now, I was back to being on my own. The survivor within had awoken in the sea tonight and I knew I needed time to figure this all out but knowing we could stay in this beautiful home with this beautiful soul and with Nana nearby I would make it once again. I knew I was holding on to someone very special and to be blessed in this short life with two men who had wanted to safeguard me and be a part of my life was an amazing piece of luck.

"Marcus" I said into his chest, "can you be patient with me? Tonight has just been so crazy and although he hurt me like none other I feel I owe him some mourning and to put him into the ground considering all the bad things that happened in the end." I pulled out of the hug and looked up at him.

He looked deep into my eyes, "He scarred you Soleil, you don't owe him anything! He almost killed you, why would you owe him anything? I don't understand." He said sorrowfully and with anger.

I pulled completely away from him now, he didn't get it. Brody had saved my life once, Marcus hadn't listened at all. Brody had found me as a kid and looked after me, took responsibility for me. He taught me how to find food, love music, clean my clothes...everything. He had been my parents, friend, lover and soulmate. The least I could do was wait until he was cold in the ground before I opened my heart up completely to someone new. Marcus had been amazing, but it was like he wasn't paying much attention to anything. If he had looked hard enough he would have seen my scars before. If he had listened to what I did say instead of noting my times of silence maybe he would have learned something about me. Maybe because tonight my dress had revealed me to him and he liked what he saw he now wanted me. He always had a reputation as a play boy, he always had his latest fling on his arm on the red carpets or was seen devouring her in the VIP section of the hottest club.

I took another step away, he could end up back on the drugs, he could end up just like Brody, maybe he only let us stay because he took pity on us or wanted some kind of sexual favour in return! He said he didn't know me, but really what did I know of him. I felt cold all of a sudden. I wanted to get away. Two minutes ago his embrace had been all I craved and it brought me so much comfort but now I didn't want him to touch me; I didn't want to look at him. I started to feel panicked, I felt twelve years old again, like when I got caught sleeping in my mom's neighbor's garage. She had been furious but felt so much pity she threw me a Twinkie and told me to fuck off. I ran out of that garage scared she would tell my mom or release her dog on me. But I ran, I ran and ran till I found myself behind the gym at school. I had sat there, made sure I was alone then slowly started to unwrap the bar of gold she had thrown at me. I was one bite into my breakfast when Brody came round the corner, he eye was swollen shut and he had a cut over his other eye. I remember being stunned at how swollen his eye was but I knew who and why it had happened. I broke the twinkie in half as he slid down the wall next to me. I gave him the half I hadn't bitten into and we savoured our sweet treat for as long as possible in silence.

Marcus would never understand something like that, he never would understand that as important as music is, silence is sometimes just as beautiful. I didn't feel like reliving my past and all the trials and tribulations I had endured to anyone again, I didn't want to feel like I owed anyone anything. I wanted our RV back, I wanted to park up by the beach and watch the kids run on the sand every day. I wanted to keep us away from the world, safe, loved and protected. I had felt that could be exactly what we could have here, with Marcus and Dani but now I wasn't so sure.

"Marcus, the sun is coming up. I think I should go back to the house and figure out what to tell the kids. I don't know what happened last night, I'm sorry I was so emotional and all over the place. I just, I just.. I don't know.. I guess I'm just sorry." I said not looking at him but with a deliberate coldness injected into my tone. I didn't wait for his reply, I turned away and started walking quickly up the steps towards the house. I didn't look back once and prayed he would not follow me closely, my head was a mess. Half of me wanted to run back to his embrace, the other half mourned the death of my friend who no one would remember, no one would care had died except me. His life touched mine and mine alone, he had had a purpose when he had been my Brody. The children had been a product of this union but even they didn't know what we had survived before they came along. I would mourn for him, I would take time and acknowledge the life that had been lived. It had been a wonderful life, despite the ending and despite the reason it existed. I looked up at the house, squared my shoulders against my fate once again and walked even faster.

CHAPTER SIXTEEN

As soon as I came back into the house, I smelled coffee; I remembered Nana was staying and I almost ran into the kitchen. She was sat at the table with a strong cup of coffee and holding her head like she had a hangover.

“Nana?” I almost whispered, afraid I was about to burst into tears.

She swung around and her face was a mess. She took one look at me and burst into tears.

“Nana, what’s wrong? Why are you crying?” I asked urgently as she was scaring me.

“Rigo just called Mija, he told me what happened last night. Then you, what have you done to yourself Soleil? Where have you been all night?!” she was slightly frantic and pointing at my bedraggled appearance.

I ran over to her as she stood up and threw my arms around her. Deep harsh sobs found their way out of me into her chest, I crumpled and she held me, sitting on the floor rocking me and stroking my head. She started praying over me and just rocked me like a baby. Soon the sobs stopped and my throat was dry and exhausted, she continued to rock me and stroke my hair.

"Mija, what will you do now? The children will be awake soon, what do we tell them?" she asked with worry in her voice.

"I don't know Nana, what do I do now?" I asked her as I pulled away and searched out her wise eyes.

She grabbed my shoulders and forced our faces together. "Mija, I will not mourn Brody, I am not sad he is gone. He terrorised you and the babies and I will never forgive that. But I remember when you first moved in, I remember how he used to look at you and care for all three of you. He had a heart once, he loved you. You could see life had bonded you both and I know you had no one else. But he took steps away from you Mija, he did what he could to make life hard for you and the children. You remember the night he left I told you, you could cry that night but no more, you were not to spend your days crying over what had happened and definitely not over losing him. You remember?" she asked forcefully. I nodded in agreement with tears streaming down my face.

"So what are you doing now? Are these tears for him or for you? You have two children who will look to you now mija, they need to draw from your strength. They need you to be sure that a future exists for you all and it is a bright and wonderful future, free of fear and pain. Look where you have brought them, Sol. Look how happy they are here. You have always done right by them, so let Brody go now. He made it easy for you by dying and now you are truly free, only your memories will haunt you so long as you let them." She still held my eyes, my tears reflected in her own, but now she smiled broadly and started to stand holding me up and encouraging me to stand.

"Nana, I just came in from the beach. Marcus found me there earlier. He said we can stay here as long as we want to Nana. We spoke very openly too, he has feelings for me Nana, he wants to be a part of our life. He said he wants to erase my scars..." I looked searchingly into her eyes, like a child I sought guidance and reassurance from her, I wanted her to tell me what to do, I was lost in emotion and panic was rising inside me. I didn't know what to believe, I didn't have the first idea what my next step would be but knew very soon both Marcus and the children would be here with us and this is not what I wanted them to see. I shook Nana's arms to harshly,

"Nana, tell me! What do I do ? Where do I go? I have nothing of my own Nana, I feel like I am half a human right now. I want to scream and fight and run but just moments ago Marcus held me and I felt so calm" my grip eased as I remembered the sound of the sea mirroring the sound of his heart as I rested my tired mess on his chest, resting and calm.

"You looks like you did 10 years ago except not scared anymore, confident and knowledgeable enough to survive. You stand tall and walk strong mija, you are not wrong when you follow your heart. Do what is best for the kids first, then see what else needs to be fixed. Kids first" she ordered.

Marcus joined us in the kitchen, he looked worried and was slightly out of breath. He was looking from me to Nana, seeking an insight, asking questions of us both.

I turned to Nana, "Nana, we are going to go away for a few nights and I will tell them what has happened. I don't know what will happen..." I stopped short when I heard Marcus draw in his breath and prayed he wouldn't interrupt me. I turned to look at him and his face was a mess. His face was dread, fear, tired, old; it was shocking to behold.

“Marcus” I said with as much care as I could feel, “I need to go make this ok with them first and foremost, I will be back and we will fix the rest but first the kids. You can understand that right. Whichever way they go, I go. That’s just natural. You get that surely?”

He starred at me repeating his proclamations and questions like a firestorm through his beautiful burnt oak eyes. I knew he was sincere, but to move forward I had to bury the past and make sure Lily and Jason were happy and not distressed by all that had happened in such a short space of time. I had a plan, where I would go and what we would do, but I couldn’t share it with anyone. It was private; some things you just need to do, get done and pack away. We all needed some space, things had become intense very quickly and space would give us a chance to breathe deep and make sure our footing was grounded. No more surprises, open hearts, open doors, open to change. I deliberately brought Nana back into the scene. Staring at her I reassured her, “We will be okay Nana, going to use some garage sale money to treat the kids and break the news. I will call you.” I gave her a big hug and kissed her cheek.

“Once the kids wake up can you give them some breakfast and I will back our bags we need to get going. Shall I drop you home first Nana?” I put on my supermom voice like I was planning the drive to school.

“Don’t worry about us Soleil. Rigo will come for us soon, I will just help Marcus clean up a little, if that’s okay with you Marcus?” she asked.

“Ya,” his voice cracked “Sure Nana, you can stay as long as you like. Soleil, will you be okay? Can I do anything?”

“You have done so much already, no we will be fine, just some time away. It will be good for everyone.” I answered assuredly.

The kids bounded into the kitchen with Dani bouncing alongside them when they stopped dead in their tracks.

“Ma, what are you wearing?! You and Marcus are matching!” Lily gasped.

They both starred at me in silence, even Dani stayed still.

“So guys, I have a surprise for you besides my clothes and I need you to have a huge breakfast and get dressed for an adventure! What do you think?" I asked overexcitedly, very likely down to near panic.

"Where to Ma?" Jason asked heading towards Nana and breakfast.

I stepped in front of him and gave him a big hug. "We will have a blast, honestly, you guys have been so good lately and me and Nana think you enjoy a treat!"

Lily moved over to the table with a quizzical look on her face, she knew something was underfoot but she stayed calm and knew I would always do what is best. She looked at me and I smiled at her looking deep into her basalt eyes. She smiled back and I knew she trusted me and would be ready for whatever was next.

CHAPTER SEVENTEEN

About forty-five minutes later we were on the road and my hand reached out to turn on the radio but reconsidered. The kids had eaten and dressed and were ready but they had no idea for what. I had promised fun which was sure to happen but I also had to tell them their father was gone. He had left traces of himself in them, he had gifted them the best of himself and they were absolute treasures. They must be slightly scared, I thought, they need to know something; I cleared my throat.

"Ok, so are you ready for the big reveal?" I asked in my sneaky spy voice. "Do you want to know what the mission is?"

"YES!!" came the chorus, a mix of joy, curiosity and excitement.

"We are finally making that trip you wanted to ..."

"DISNEYLAND!!??" they looked at each other in shock.

"Yes, we are finally going to the big D. I have two nights booked at the Disneyland Hotel and two days of passes for us. Fireworks are ready and the best pool you can imagine! How does that sound?" They burst into squeals of delight and started talking over each other excitedly. I turned on the radio now that I knew they were excited and I made sure to motor a bit faster.

After checking in and collecting their jaws off the floor, we headed towards the park. It was still early and we hit all the rides the kids had only ever heard about. The kids could not stop gasping and shrieking every time something new came into view. I was exhausted by the time we sat down for some dinner near the Pirate ride. The kids were starving but desperate to get back to the rides. I reminded them to slow down because I wasn't going on any rides for at least thirty minutes after we'd eaten.

"What time are the fireworks Ma?" Jason asked between bites.

"10pm little man, you know we can go back to the room and watch them from the balcony if you are tired?" I asked innocently, knowing there was no way he was leaving the park early.

"No way! I am wide awake and ready for anything! Remember you told us you had found the best place to watch the fireworks when you came here before? Do you think we can watch from there too?" he asked seriously as he wanted the maximum experience possible and was relying on my one day of experience to make that happen. I chuckled to myself.

"You know what, I remember exactly where it is and if we move a little early we will be able to claim it and have a five-minute rest before the show starts. How about that?" I proposed.

"Yes please! Lily what do you think?" he turned and gave her his full attention.

She was sitting quietly, just looking around her and taking in everything. She also looked longingly at a family sitting next to us and then she smiled at herself and looked at Jason realising he was speaking to her.

"What did you say Jay? I was thinking of something funny." She giggled.

"Well share it with us then so we can giggle, lovely" I pressed, curious what her thoughts were after such a brilliant day.

"It was when I went shopping with Marcus yesterday, we did the special shopping then went to Trader Joe's to get the normal stuff. SO we are wearing our funny wigs and we get to the cashier and he says to Marcus 'Wow, you are cool man, you let your daughter have pink hair!' So Marcus laughed and said 'Nah, she was born with it'. Ma, you should have seen the cashier's face! We were laughing so hard when we got to the car!" she continued to laugh at her story with Jason rocking beside her.

"You had pink hair Lily?!" he asked her shocked. She nodded and laughed even harder which encouraged him to do the same just imagining it. I smiled to myself, I was struck by the idea that Lily, Jason and Marcus had also shared some memories and that they enjoyed spending time together.

I had not thought about Marcus since we left the house. I had not wanted to think about Marcus since we left the house. Now I was thinking about Marcus. I imagined what the story Lily told must have looked like or felt like. They had fun; she felt safe and enjoyed herself. He was kind by nature, kind by default and he had really embraced what he said he would do and had not invaded any personal space or barriers. I wondered what he was doing now, had Nana actually gone home or were they finishing the tequila from the party? Suddenly I realised I felt freer knowing I had an option with Marcus and knowing we were welcome to stay where we were and be free of the stress of homelessness. But it was so much more than that. He genuinely wanted to know me and take time in doing so. He had made no advances or even proposed a handshake. He had merely accepted me how I was and recognized I was damaged and perhaps quick to flight. So he provided a shelter from the storm and warmth and kindness which was slowly restoring me to strength and allowing me the chance to produce my finest work yet. In a few days a bit more of my truth would be out there and the film I made released. Marcus meant something to me and I found myself wanting to live life alongside someone like him, a strong person who knows himself and can face life head-on with you not dragging you from behind. At that moment I saw him as potentially the best friend I could ask for; a companion, reliability. Who knew what would lie ahead, but tonight I had one very hard task to carry out, but a fitting one. I would tell the kids about Brody but we would celebrate the goodness, the happy moments and the memories we would take forward because they enhanced our lives not hindered them.

"Finish up guys, we have about two hours before we need to get to our spot." I said popping a fry into my mouth and shaking away thoughts of Marcus.

We visited the jungle, space, fantasy and went downtown. Our thoughts stayed focused on absorbing every moment of our day which was sweetened by knowing we could do it all again tomorrow. We laughed and hugged a lot and got a chance to really catch up while we waited in line for our next adventure. It was blessed time, truly blessed. We had money for treats and genuinely had nothing but fun on our minds. We were free, in that all worry was gone, we had everything we needed at arm's reach.

After getting in a parade, ice creams and pictures with princesses, I started walking towards the castle. I reached out for their hands and retraced an old route travelled only once before.

It was the weekend and when we woke up, Brody told me to hurry as he had a surprise for me. He was almost giddy and I was so curious what he had been up to. We came into the front room and his grandad was getting his coat on, he nodded emotionlessly at us, "You two comin then?" he smirked.

"Yes please grandad, we will make our own way back home so you don't have to worry, I got keys too, Sir." Brody said politely.

"Hmm, ya, that's good" he replied while nodding his head and reaching for his wallet, pulling it out and opening it. Yesterday had been payday so there were plenty of bills on display "Take this, boy, have a good day. I ain't never worried bout you, this will probably be the only time I ever get to treat you now so take this; enjoy your day" He shoved a wad of bills at Brody but didn't once look at his astonished face.

My mind was racing, but completely intrigued, what did we need all that cash for? Where were we going? Turns out grandad got a job pouring concrete at Disneyland. They go in about opening time and there was a narrow path that took you right in at Splash Mountain, and into the Happiest Place on Earth for free. As we walked out onto the Park I could not believe we were here. It was an awesome sight to behold but we knew we had one day so we ran to make the most of it. We ended up by the castle when the fireworks started and it was beautiful. We lay down on the concrete and grass looking up; we were partially hidden so no one seemed to bother us and it was like having the entire show to yourself. We held hands and just took in the magnificence we both knew would be fleeting, but always ones to get their money's worth, we were watching each bulb explode with delight. In silence, we each recorded our own version of the moment and finally felt rewarded for surviving, being strong and not giving up. It was perfect.

We reached the spot and it was exactly as it had been that day. You could take a few steps off the path and there was another path that no one seemed to use as it wound tightly against a huge stone planter with large ferns covering the soil. I sat Jason up on the stone wall and reached for my backpack. I opened it and produced the two pieces of the love heart I had kept. Lily gasped in what sounded like horror. I looked down at her face and saw she was staring wide eyed at the heart, fists clenched.

"Is he back Mama, did he come back?" she whispered with trembling lips.

I bent down and gathered her up in my arms, hugging her tightly and stood up. I didn't expect such an adverse reaction. In fact, I had never realised how they felt about the thought of Brody coming back but I knew I had to do this. We had to face the truth and the new journey that lie ahead. I gently sat Lily down next to Jason on the wall and faced them both. I handed them each a piece of the heart and held their hands.

"Listen guys, I have to tell you something that is difficult but not scary. It is a good thing and maybe one day you will feel differently about it but today has been an amazing day and one we can keep in our hearts forever. But, something major has changed and I want you to feel anything you want to feel and say anything you want to say when I tell you what's happened ok?" They shook their hands in the affirmative; I took in a deep breath and continued their eyes wide with concern, "Yesterday, when I left the party, I had to go to the hospital. I had to go to the hospital because Pa was there." Lily's eyes shot open as wide as an oreo and she sucked in her breath sharply as tears started to form.

"Yes, he was there, but the thing is you see... he.. he was there because, well he isn't sick, no, um he is gone... he died... I am so sorry guys, I just knew you needed to know." I said to a wall of silence, as still as the wall they were sitting on. They didn't move or speak, I was checking to see if they were even breathing. Jason suddenly looked at Lily almost to ask permission to speak first. She met his stare and nodded, a stern expression on her face. He looked at me and then down at his feet.

"Ma, is it ok if we are not really sad right now? I mean we just had a magical day and it was fun because it was just us. Pa would have been grumpy by now and instead we are here having the best day ever." He stopped, not knowing what else to say or even sure he communicated what he was feeling properly. Lily took up the baton and cleared her throat.

"I think he means, it is ok Ma. Pa left us a while ago and left you really bad. If he is gone then you are safe and we would have you over him any day. Thank you for telling us this way Ma, for bringing us here and then giving us this news. We are all free now, we cannot be hurt anymore. We love you Ma." They both threw open their arms and we had a huge, hard hug. Tears streamed down my face and they both felt so relaxed and cuddly once again. I held on to them and made sure they felt just how much I needed them, I felt their strength and love resonate and my tears turned to those of joy and gratitude.

I pulled back from the embrace as the first announcement went, fireworks in three minutes.

"Ok guys, this is the plan. We will bury the heart in the fern planter behind you ok. We will leave our memory of Pa here to enjoy the show every night and send him off with one last little bit of love. We had good times, and great times. You have to take the positive forward ok, promise me you will each bury your half with a good memory attached to it. Your dad loved you guys so much and when you were little he spent his whole day playing with you and helping you explore. He taught you both so much and loved you so much, he never slept when you were born, constantly checking on you and just staring at you. We had so much fun and meeting Nana too. So, let's do that ok? Let's send him off tonight and then we will only take good memories away with us as we start a new life in a new home." I watched their faces change and smiles return to their lips. "Are you ready kids, can we do this? Lily? Jason?" I asked staring intently at both of their faces, eager to know what their thoughts were.

Lily looked down at her half of the heart and traced the letter L with her finger. She smiled and closed her eyes then turned to the plants behind her and started digging a little hole. Jason followed her lead and silently kissed his half and turned to help Lily dig.

"Do you want to say good bye Ma?" Lily asked and I thought my heart would burst. This was good bye, she was absolutely right. No more torment, no more lying and covering. Just the truth laid out there for us to live, the road paved with maybes and what ifs would be ours but we walked strong together and valued the companions we were blessed with. I moved forward and placed my hands over the heart. I silently thanked him and prayed he would finally find peace, I kissed both kids and motioned at them to finish the task and bury the past.

Music filled the air and excitement was high, the fireworks began gently and over the tower of the castle, reds, blue and white exploded across the sky. I stood between the children and held them close, we felt solid, we felt like we had each other to face the future with. Today was a good day, great even; we had sent off the last of our love and wishes with Brody now and knew this moment was our spectacular, we watch each exploding bulb shooting higher and higher, ready to show the world what we had inside. Brody's last gift to us, an ignition, reason to strive forward and enjoy what goodness we had been blessed with and relinquish the negativity and hurt to the past, a place we no longer called home or had any desire to rebuild.

CHAPTER EIGHTEEN

Waking up to the sound of surf and seagulls, I walked out onto our beach hut patio. We had spent our second day at Disneyland in the pool of the hotel in the morning then we went back to the park until closing, this time taking in the firework show from the banks of the American River where we waved off the characters and saw the water show. From there I drove straight to Malibu and checked us into this beautiful beach hut resort. I wanted to really give the kids a treat especially as I had a meeting today, so Rigo was coming with Nana to have a luxury beach day. I planned to stay one more night here before going back to Marcus', I thought a little space and time would be good for everyone, especially as today was the day of the big release and I had to get down to the record label for all the finalities and to make sure the band actually approved it too. I was nervous but not worried. Johan promised I could stay in the tech booth during the premiere and that I didn't have to meet the band or anyone. Johan agreed when I said I was nervous about their feedback and would just watch their reactions in case they didn't like it from afar as he was the business man and the one who could fix any problems.

I had entertained thoughts of Marcus over the last few days and intermixed with good memories of Brody and smiles from the kids I was feeling positive. The kids had spoken briefly about Brody and we had a conversation about how he died and retold some stories from the happy times. I told the kids that one day we could go see where his grave is if they wanted to and both agreed that it might be a good idea when they are older, because right now they were still a little sad and angry with him. I knew it would take time, effectively he had left without saying goodbye to them and he left them scared. Time was the best healer and would be what we would use to firmly set our feet down onto the right path again.

My meeting was at 11:00 but I wanted to get there a little early so I wouldn't run into any of the band members. I knew it was silly, but I wanted them to watch the film free of any knowledge that it was some way connected to me or Marcus. I was slightly worried they would think I used Marcus by moving in to make the film better but the proof this was untrue was in the film and it would speak for itself.

The kids ran outside and looked out over the beach, they had already been down to test the water and were running around looking for shells. "Hey beautiful" a familiar voice called out. I turned to see Rigo giving me his brightest smile and Nana keeping pace in her sunhat and sliders. Rigo was loaded down with a huge cooler, towels and a chair. It felt amazing to see them and it felt good to feel happy and safe once again. I walked up to Nana and threw my arms around her.

"Good to see you Nana, really, really good to see you." I whispered to her and held her tight.

"Hey, Sol, you got a hug for me sis?" Rigo interrupted and gave me a nudge. I turned and looked at him, flashing him my biggest smile, "Of course I do brother!" I turned and jumped on him with arms wide open. "How are you doing? SO good to see you today!"

"We are good sis, I am happy to see you smiling you know, and even happier you booked us a day in this place!" he let out a low whistle, "Sol you gone big here girl, this is nice!"

"I always wanted to come stay here ever since I used to clean the place after school back in the day. I hope you guys have a rad day bro, there is an open tab for food and drinks and you have towels and toys and all sorts. I need to get going, traffic is shit this time, but hey it is a beautiful day right?" I realized I had gone corporate on him so I laughed, "Sorry Rigo, I just want to get this over with you know, show my film and be like chill. This will pay me a sick amount and then I can figure out the next step. You know it's like the stress will be off my back. I just hope they like it."

"The film is sick Sol, it is perfect. It celebrates the group and everything they have done, you will be fine. If they don't like it then they are idiots, that track you wrote is deep as well, really gives the montage part some emotion. It's good, Sol, honestly, it's good. Don't worry" he pulled out of the hug and held my shoulders, looking deep into my eyes. I held his stare and silently reassured him I was okay, that the other night was dealt with for now.

"I told the kids, Rigo, they know. I had to tell them, I don't want to lie and to be honest they are free of fear from him now and that was something I didn't realise it would do. The second day at Disney we just had a blast and they were little again, just silly, you know. It was good." I explained.

"That's good Sol, I am glad you guys had some time together and just having fun. We are going to have loads of fun today, you go and do what you need to do. Open tab , ha, ta loca, Nana packed a feast, said the kids hadn't eaten in two days!" he laughed out loud "See how worried we are about your lack of cooking skills!"

I laughed as I realised that the cooler was actually huge and looked fully loaded, These two had genuinely made my day and I could not wait to be back this afternoon to enjoy it all with them.

"Alright bro, you have fun and I will call you when I am done. Keep an eye on Jason in the water ok. Bye Nana, Bye Kids!" I shouted across to her and the kids as she had already gathered them up in a big hug and was chatting away.

"Hey, today is a beautiful day, why don't you take my convertible today. Enjoy a cool ride and arrive in style at your meeting." He chucked me the keys and smiled "Seriously, go get what is yours in style hermana."

I looked down at the keys to his beloved Mustang convertible, his midnight black and blue Mustang. I loved this car and the noise it made. A huge smile spread across my face and I chucked him my car keys, "Just in case you need a ride, ok?

Thanks Rigo, this is amazing. I love you bro." I gave him one last hug and a kiss on the cheek and skipped off towards his little beast. "Thank you Rigo!" I shouted as I jumped in the driver's seat and turned the key.

"Go easy Soleil, I ain't messing, she comes back in one piece or you are finished, understand?" I revved the engine in response, and waved back at him.

I turned onto the small road leading to the gates and smiled, Rigo was right, I was going to go get my success in style. I knew I had produced an amazing piece of film and if they didn't want it I was sure it would go for a good price to any of the music channels when their anniversary came up. I put both hands on the wheel and drove out through the gate onto my destiny.

I arrived at the headquarters of the label and passed the keys to the valet. It was the first time any of the valets walked up to my car instead of waving me on so I figured I might as well use them; besides they were better at parking then me and I didn't want to put a scratch on Rigo's baby.

I walked into the building and walked tall to Johan's office. He looked at me in shock, "Soleil my dear what the fuck happened to you? Did you have a fight with a pair of scissors?" he laughed at his own joke and took a sip of his coffee.

"Ha, ha Johan, how are you? Nah, just wearing my hair up these days, nothing to hide anymore, no biggie." I responded monotone, Johan's dumbass jokes were not doing anything to settle my nerves, so I got straight to the point. "I am going to the sound booth, ok, if you need me I'll be hiding in there till they see it and love it."

"Ah, confidence mon chere, good to see. Your film will do the talking Soleil dear, you just go and hide like you asked and watch minds be blown away!" he blew me a kiss and took another sip of his coffee.

I walked down the hall to the stairs leading up to the sound booth where we would control the film as it sat at the back of the small private theatre they had custom built. No one except Kevin was in the booth, he never had an assistant, he just got on with the job and was super experienced and confident so no one ever questions the quality he would produce.

"Hey Kev, it's just me. I am going to sit here to watch but don't worry I won't touch anything!" I smiled and pulled up a chair closer to the window.

"Hey Soleil, how are you? Good to see you here. Ya no problem dude, you sit and chill, I have everything set up.

"Cool, just ignore me Kevin, I am a little nervous, you do what you have to do and I won't make a sound." I told him as I didn't want him to think I was being rude.

"No worries Sol, I get it. But if it is any consolation I think your film is really sick. I am a huge fan of theirs and watching the film took me back decades! Right back to my first concert, you had footage of it in there. SO awesome, honestly any fan will love it." He gushed excitedly.

"Thanks Kev, that's real sweet. Honestly, that is what I hoped would happen for the fans." I looked back at him and smiled, suddenly calmer and just human again; grateful.

People started coming into the theatre, executives and then strode in Willow, followed by Marcus and Hope. They were dressed nice but still enjoying themselves and catching up on things since Friday. Hugo, walked in with a cup of something and his bass. He showed off his lightly bandaged finger then said something the other band members laughed at making their way to the front row of the theatre and sitting down.

Johan strolled in from behind the screen, his hands clasped in front of him, smiling knowingly and then waving to someone in the back. He walked towards the band and shook hands with Marcus, smiling even wider. There was a short conversation and some other execs came in and took seats at the back. I looked back at Kevin,

"How long til we start Kev?" I adjusted my chair and moved a little further from the window, suddenly conscious that this was potentially the moment when my work would be exhibited in front of people whose opinion really mattered to me.

"Two minutes to air" he announced into his mic to all those with headsets on the floor. The ushers started cajoling everyone to a seat and Johan jumped back onto the stage and clapped his hands.

"Ladies and Gentlemen, welcome, welcome to a celebration of 25 glorious years of music, creativity, chaos, loss and love. Always Love. We start today with the first screening of a short film documenting the journey of Hugo, Hope, Willow and Marcus....Zephyr!" he waved his arm towards the screen and the lights went down. I sat still and waited, eight minutes and forty-eight seconds til I know if all the work I did is a success, til I know we are covered for a few months and possibly more. The screen lit up and the soundtrack started, this was it. Nine minutes.

The film evoked claps and cheers; at times I didn't expect such a strong reaction but I guess images we saw would always be interpreted differently to the ones who had lived all of those moments and had them as living memories not just a second captured in one frame. The band were sitting as close as possible and smiling, seeing images of their hectic past and the loving and diverse family that they grew. Their own music was stellar as usual and towards the end over a ninety-second montage of the band with their families and loved ones and shots from their youth and high school my song was due to come on. I kind of hoped the images would overpower the music and not gain too much interest as I was nervous on how it would be received. The execs had been happy with it, they didn't realise it was my own work and were happy with the harmony and mood it set over the short montage. I knew the exact moment the song would start and I closed my eyes as it started.

For-ward, four-ward, ahead we move

Laughter, love and peace to soothe

Like the sun and the moon, push pull

Tiredness, sadness, whatever is due

The push pull, push pull with you...

Ninety seconds later, I opened my eyes as a hard rock song cut in and injected the energy back into the film, the celebration, the finale. Immediately I realised Marcus was sat back against his chair; he wasn't smiling, just staring at the screen with an almost blank face. I was confused, he didn't seem to be enjoying the film anymore. Willow turned to him and tapped his shoulder saying something to him. A baby picture of Hope naked with a ukulele popped up on the screen and both started laughing, Willow turning to Hope and bellowing. Soon it appeared the energy was restored and they watched the finale together, with arms around each other. Johan was smiling like a cat and the execs looked happy too. The record people started clapping to the end track and soon the entire theatre was clapping, rocking to the film's finale. I couldn't hold in my smile; they loved it and I had done it. I would survive just like them; another twenty-five years and then I will make my own film. Yes! I was thrilled; I turned to Kevin and grinned.

"Smashed it Sol, absolutely fuckin smashed it out the park!" he leaned towards me for a fist bump.

I laughed as we had a fist bump, he was right, it was good, really, really good. This would sell as well and that royalty would set us up nice for at least two years until the hype died down around their anniversary. I had a chance to move on now, I had a chance to secure a future for us and settle the kids down freed from burdens and worry.

I went to sit back down but caught a glimpse of myself in the window and stopped. A red scar had settled like a noose around the left side of my neck; like a reminder to stay alert, stay on track and not fall victim again to the darker realms of life which can hang you and steal life from you and destroy the fragile soul and lead one astray. The feeling I had felt on the beach that night returned and I felt wary again, dubious of this life and where my place would be in all of this, would I just fall victim to a different sort of control. There was no way to hide this mark, unless I took to wearing turtlenecks in the summer, no, unfortunately this would be a reminder that marked me and it would have to be worn and unexplained. I didn't owe anyone anything now, what Marcus had asked for was exactly what needed to be protected and guarded. I owed no one an explanation, I owed no one a dime and I definitely didn't owe anyone my time. I knew I had told Marcus I didn't want to leave but to stay now would be dangerous. He wanted to know me, know me?! There was no way I wanted to spend the rest of my life explaining how life had dragged me across the stones and back again. Brody had known all of these things and knew how it all made me feel and how I had to deal with it. Those memories had gone with him now, only the good remained of this I made sure, therefore there was no need to go back in time with someone when all I wanted to do was move forward. Marcus had been exceptional, he had welcomed us, hosted us, cared for us and committed to providing a home for longer. He was amazing with the kids and they trusted him and were always relaxed with him. He brought out good qualities in them and evoked confidence in them, he was always kind to me and respectful of my space and privacy.

It had felt safe in his arms, his embrace was so caring, so warm yet not demanding, he held me and I rested, I was calm, at peace. He was just two steps ahead of where I needed to be to stay on with him. I was not in the same position as him to enjoy something new and demanding, I needed to settle the kids, find a school and find the next project. I just felt like I could not give Marcus what he wanted even though it wasn't actually a lot in return for what he offered in exchange. Ah! It was frustrating me, it felt like a circle, the perfect future but a big price to pay from my soul. How much would partnering with a legend like Marcus cost me? What would happen when a mom and two kids get boring, doesn't fit the mould or inspire new music? I didn't even think I had any emotion left to put into any new relationship, I was drained from reactionary living and his world was a million miles from mine. What if he asked me to go to a red-carpet gig with him, what if we get spotted together and have to deal with paparazzi? I had no experience of that life, I had toured and moved around and been the media but I had never garnered any interest from anyone to be investigated or become a person of interest. Honestly, it was like a merry go round in my head, I stared into my own eyes and saw the confusion written all over my face and the anguish of the last few days still lingering in my eyes. I soon realised there was a lot of movement in the theatre except for Marcus, he was sat still in the front row still staring at the blank screen.

Awoken from my self-reflective stupor, I watched him slowly get up and look around. Suddenly, he located his target and walked straight up to Johan and spoke to him, interrupting another man who looked to be mid-flow. Johan looked surprised by whatever Marcus said and shook his head. Marcus spoke again and Johan looked straight up at the booth he knew I was sitting in. He shook his head again and put his hand on Marcus' chest in a joking manner. Marcus pushed his arm away and spoke and I could only imagine raising his voice. He continued and motioned over Sebastien, a young trainee at the record label, to come over to him. As soon as he was next to him, Marcus put his arm around him and spoke gently to him. Sebastien smiled and nodded in agreement with whatever he said and soon he was walking away and towards the exit. Marcus smiled at Johan who had a slightly panicked look on his face and had already glanced up at the booth at least twice. I suddenly had a bad feeling in my stomach and I heard the door open.

"Hey Kev, you good?"

"Hey Seb, what's up bro? You get kicked out again?" Kevin responded and chuckled.

"Funny Bro, not here to see you actually. Hey Soleil, how are the kids?" Seb spoke to me casually as he had no idea of what I had seen.

"Hey Seb, ya I am good, kids are good. How are you doing? Did you see the film?" I asked just as casually.

"Film was dope, honestly loved all of it. You did a great job everyone in there is loving it! Marcus sent me up here to find you, he wants to talk to you" he said probably thinking I would start flapping like a groupie.

"He asked for me Seb? How did he even know I was here?! Fucking Johan!" I grunted completely taken aback that Marcus knew I was even here.

"Well he didn't ask for you by name but he said he wanted to meet the person that wrote the song, you know, about the push/pull that played. He really loved it and wanted to hear the rest of the song. He asked me if I knew the person and if they were here. I said yes to both questions and said I would go and bring that person and it is you. So no he doesn't know YOU are here but knows the musician who wrote the song is, make sense?" he finished blabbering almost out of breath and surprised by my reaction. "I am sorry Soleil, have

I messed up? I didn't say a name, so he doesn't know it is you, honestly I had no idea, I thought you would be happy, this could be a great chance! You made the film and the song, he loves it! You could get another gig off the back of this no problem!" he continued trying to fill my silence but he was barely penetrating my thoughts.

He loved the song, Marcus, the legendary songwriter loved my song. This was such a shock because I had seen his reaction to the piece and he had been sitting there reflective again and slightly lost. He had recovered quickly but I could not believe that he had paid the music such great attention. There was no way I could meet him now, if he knew it was me he might launch into a declaration of admiration and shower me with praise, yet all of that seemed unnecessary, I had seen what Sebastien had now explained and I understood that he had heard my lyrics, he had felt a push pull; had ridden the mellow harmony alongside the images and had been touched. There was no need for anyone to know it was me. If they pressed they would probably find out I had made the film, but that was bound to happen anyways as I had planned to tell Marcus immediately the next time I saw him regardless. No, I could not face that room right now, I had my reward and congratulations in silence, this was enough for me. Yes, further success could easily be attained if I walked into the theater and had a turn at the showbiz folly, however, with Marcus in the room the exit price would be disruptive and was a situation I did not want to endure right now. I wanted to go back to the hut, have dinner with my lovelies and tell them all about the screening. I needed reassurance that the reality I knew was still real, that the relationships that formed me and supported me still stood strong. I realised Sebastien and Kevin were both staring at me, but I knew what I had to do.

"Tell them the person left already." I looked Seb straight in the eyes, picked up my bag and walked out the door straight out across the parking lot to the valet, not once looking back, I would deal with all that when I wanted to, but not right now, I knew where I needed to be.

CHAPTER NINETEEN
MARCUS

I walked back towards the house slowly, knowing it was empty and I had no idea when it would be full again. I never thought I would care so much or so quickly. I really enjoyed having them in the house and living with their energy and simplicity. Time had passed quickly and today Hugo got the all clear to start practicing again, so in a few weeks we could be off. Eight months away, hotels. airplanes. sound-checks and filming. For the first time in twenty-five years I had no desire to tour. I just wanted to stay at home, stay closer to Soleil and her family and this new found awesomeness that filled every day of my life.

I was absolutely gobsmacked when I learned that Soleil had created the film. The songwriter I was after had left early but I had a suspicion it was her. She was probably there, Johan let it slip as we left that he would tell her I enjoyed the show. I couldn't believe it, she was soul trembling talented. A master of image and sound, her melody had instantly touched my inner being. Push Pull, push pull with you...it meant so much, it captured the give and take, the support and the weakness, the good the bad; they push and pull each other like the sun pushes the moon from the sky to brighten the day and bring forth the uncertain night; the future. It was awesome, truly awesome, she had captured the fundamental basic foundation of life in such a brief yet powerful song. I prayed I was right and it was Soleil, I would love to hear the rest of the song. I opened the front door and Dani slowly gantered towards me not wagging her tail wildly like she normally did.

"I miss them too babe, me too.." I told her as I bent down and stroked her giving her a hug. I stood up and flung my helmet down, the noise slightly reassuring and space filling. Sylvia had been in, that was clear. Poor dear she had a bit more to do than normal, I still had things left out from Saturday. Saturday. That was a day it all started. Getting ready for the party one minute with the enchanting Lily delighting in her pink hair then holding Soleil by the sea as the sun came up. I never imagined she would leave that day, I knew she was well because I had spoken to Rigo a few times but I missed them, there was something very missing from this home now. Holding her had been a dream, she felt perfect and tiny in my arms, like a trembling bird and her head rested right over my heart keeping it calm and steady, a bird that finally settled and trusted me to keep her safe, I wanted to hold her forever and never let go, she was a dream, an angel and deep down I knew she was made for me, I just felt connected to her in so many ways even though I knew virtually nothing about her. She filled my head when she and the kids didn't fill my days and I hoped I hadn't blown my chances. I had no way to understand why she left the way she did, she said it was because the kids needed to be told about their dad and she wanted to do that her way which I respect, admittedly I didn't understand her reaction to his loss but I knew I had to respect it, she had had a life with him, she had children with him but he had scarred her, beat her so badly she was scarred for life and then for him to die that way...

As she walked out of the door that day, I turned to look at Nana and I swear I had tears in my eyes. I was so confused, she had said she would stay but then left so abruptly, I asked Nana what was going on and she just gave me a hug and told me patience would see me right. Rigo showed up after a while and I was so grateful as I wanted him to explain to me what had happened, I didn't know what to expect. Would she be back? Would he just turn up one day and collect all of her stuff? I was almost panicked by the time we settled down on the beach with a spliff and a million questions. He sparked up and took a few long drags staring out to sea. The clouds had come in that day and the sea was almost in rebellion compared to how calm it had been hours before. Rigo didn't say anything he just stared out at the waves and embraced himself in the smoke.

"Rigo, I need your help bro. Please, I don't understand what is happening inside me and around me, I need you to be honest with me bro, I haven't got a clue about Soleil. Will she come back?" I asked with intensity and perhaps too much eagerness. I sat back a bit as he swung round quickly and stared hard at my face, almost searching for something.

"Why is that such a concern to you bro, you look messed up. Have you slept at all? Seriously, have some of this" he passed his joint over, never taking his eyes off mine, I took one drag, it immediately hit the top of my head and I rocked back a little as I exhaled.

"Ya, no I didn't sleep at all, can I tell you what happened last night Rigo? It was crazy! That scar on her neck is just there now, it just screams pain from where it winds around her neck, I saw her back too bro, I can't believe it. Why did he do that to her?" I blurted out the words and he turned his back on me.

"Have another toke bro, you are stressin. Seriously, maybe you don't need to know all of what you think you need to know. Sol's past is her own, it is what made her who she is. She never had it easy you know, never had love and safety, she just survived by the skin of her teeth" he started.

"Ya but seriously, why did he beat her like that? She looks like she was..." I interrupted only to be met rage in his eyes as he turned to face me fully.

"Was what bro?! Beaten? Whipped with a leather belt? Strangled? That is what happened, mother fucker... give me some more of that" he motioned for me to pass him the spliff. I had another pull and complied not saying a word, shocked at what he had said.

Rodrigo relived that night for my benefit and told me how Lily and Jason had run over to his house screaming and crying because they had seen Soleil thrown against the door frame and knew things were getting bad. He had run towards the house and when he walked in found her unconscious with him sitting on her choking her.

"I thought she was dead Marcus, I thought I was too late," he had tears in his eyes and I could feel his pain "five more minutes Marcus she would have been dead, seriously, dead, he had her on the floor she was covered in blood and these horrible welts. She had fought back but he was pheening, she was no match for him. I pulled him off her and punched him straight in the jaw. I started pounding his sorry ass thinking he had just killed my sister and the kids were terrified already, shit bro it was intense, I almost lost my shit completely. She woke up and spoke, it was a miracle Marcus, she sounded like she came back from the dead, like she had been somewhere else you know. Best sound I ever heard bro, you know seriously, I thought she was gone." I nodded to communicate my understanding, I was horrified, shocked and I wanted to hear the rest of the story so I stayed quiet and just nodded to encourage him to continue.

"Well, she got herself up and took herself to the bathroom.. and then.. well.." his voice suddenly cracked and he went quiet, "I'm sorry bro, I... I can't... she, well, she ...." He stopped suddenly and held his head in his hands, two deep sobs came out of his massive frame and now I was seriously intrigued. I needed to know the rest of this, I couldn't believe what I was hearing.

That night must have been horrifying for all of them. If Rigo was still this upset by it I couldn't imagine what the kids and Soleil must be feeling. She truly was all the things I thought, she must be strong, determined...a survivor, she got up and walked away from an attempt by Death to take her and carried on. She had come to me, she had presented her crazy plan and came to stay. She had been through all of that, was still treating her wounds yet she was able to get on with every day bravely and determined as though nothing had happened. She smiled and laughed with the children and joined in with all the fun but her eyes...her eyes always betrayed her, she had a sadness that sat in the corner of her eye alongside an alertness which looked like she was ready to grab the kids and run at any time. I had felt her sorrow on the beach when I held her, I wanted to protect her, I wanted to hold her against any danger and carry her over any flames that threatened her beautiful soul. I looked at Rigo, he was silent, his head was still hung low but he took another drag and sat up straighter.

“You know Marcus, I don’t know anyone like her. She is my best friend, if she is with me I feel like I can do anything. She is special bro, really special…” he said wistfully

“She definitely is!” I confirmed immediately, looking out to the sea and remembering her ethereal figure floating along singing.

“Listen, Marcus, I’m a say this one time to you and that’s it, ok. I look at you and I see a lost kid, she has intrigued you and captivated you, any idiot can see that, but she is not here to look after you understand. Whatever you want from her forget it bro, she isn’t in a position to give anything. Watching her get up every day, not giving up, amazes me but I know it takes so much out of her. She is recovering from something terrible bro and then the asshole goes and dies in this horrible way and she is literally left abandoned in the world. You see before she moved in next to us it was just them two, they were something else at the beginning, you couldn’t see where one finished and the other started! He adored her dude, he was just so awesome with her and then it changed. Brown and Charlie and all sorts of shit got back in his life and he left her for it. He got violent, moody and unpredictable. She thought she could save him but at the end realised she had to save herself and the kids. She used to tell me about their adventures as kids and their caravan on the beach, trips they took, bands they worked with and the million and one times she kept falling in love with him. They were tight bro, you never saw something like that. They were survivors, warriors, they kept to themselves, laid low and kept their business to themselves. Nana never liked him but she was always super suspicious and she always knows right about people in the end I guess" he stopped, lit his spliff and took a long pull. He passed it towards me and in my stunned stupor I accepted and took another drag.

"You see, I know you think you like her, you think she is your missing piece, but she ain't bro. She is so far from your world you bring her into it and you will make her disappear. She isn't rock star WAG material, she would never want that kind of life. She is chill, always chill but she is thinking 24/7 but you would never know. You can give her everything she needs bro and provide for the kids too of that I have no doubt but I don't think you can handle the baggage, lifestyle and parts of her that are not sunny. As bright as she shines there is a dark side to her. Sometimes she retreats into herself and her shell which you would never be able to penetrate. She probably never even gave you a hug, right?!" he asked thinking he knew the answer for sure.

"Actually," I started slowly "I held her last night Rigo. She felt perfect, it was purely a hug bro, honestly!" I explained quickly as I did not want to awaken the jealous brother beast!

"Last night?! What are you talking about? Why were you with her this last night? When I dropped her off all the lights were off, we figured you went to sleep. She told me she wanted to be alone and had a job to do. Did you sleep with her?!" He shouted the last bit, going back to being angry.

I shook my head and hands at him rapidly, "No bro, not at all! Seriously, I would have never! No way!"

"Seriously Dude , you are scaring me. Honestly. Are you in love with her? You act like she has broken your heart already, what the fuck happened last night?!" he demanded.

I launched a full account of what happened, her being in the water and then holding her. I left out the see-through dress because there was no way to explain that platonically and then I got to the part where she walked off. She walked off, just turned around and left me standing there. I knew if I followed her and asked for explanation I was unlikely going to get one and I really didn't want to upset her further. I had just sat back down put my head in my hands and tried to figure out what the hell had just happened. My story finished and I watched Rigo's face go through about three different emotions all at once.

"Shit man, she did all that? I knew I shouldn't have left her, I knew she would do something stupid. How bad did she look when she left?" he asked sombrely.

"Well to be honest she looks amazing but she tied her hair back now and that scar that just winds its way down the side of her neck, I never realised it was so bad before. I had actually thought it was a birth mark and she never swan without a t-shirt on so I was seriously shocked by her back. But when she left she looked like she had the weight of the world on her shoulders. I figured if Nana never stopped her form going, so I had no right to."

"No you would not have stopped her, no one can, she doesn't listen to anyone, she just goes on her guts, she always has. She always tells me she raised herself and so she is the only person who gets control over her life." He went silent again; I could see he was thinking hard but I was unsure how well this conversation boded for me. "Are you in love with her Marcus?" he turned his entire frame to face me as he asked me the question, "Just yes or no, I don't want no bullshit."

I stayed quiet, I had not even asked myself that question yet, I had no clear answer, there was no absolute yes or no. How could I be in love with her, I knew nothing about her, I barely knew her kids! Love her, yes, I think I did but was I in love with her already? "You know I think I love her bro, but I am not in love with her yet does that make sense?" I asked him for understanding. He nodded his head yes but said nothing so I carried on. "She is like a dream, a fantasy. She seems to command life and emanates such a powerful and enigmatic energy that I am drawn to her. I want to hold her forever and sit by her side and listen to her all at the same time. It has been such a short time she has been here but I already miss her, and the kids too! They are amazing, I never thought I would be any good around kids but we have a blast and they are so like their mother, just enchanting. I want to be around her Rigo, this is the first time I actually thought about postponing the tour just so we can spend the rest of summer together and get to know each other better. You and Nana too, I mean you guys are awesome, so loving, so kind and just so down to earth. It just feels like we have all known each other forever, it feels so natural, I can't explain it. You understand what I am saying?" almost desperate for him to something to stop my mind racing.

Rigo was staring me in the eyes now, his were slight red and puffy but I could feel his soul-piercing stare, I knew there was nothing else for me to say. I had been honest with Rodrigo and now he would tell me his truth I was sure. He would do everything in his power to safeguard the kids and Soleil, so would he let me in, would he be happy about the way I felt or would I be a threat? I had to know. "Say something, bro? Please? I just feel confused and you know her best so tell me, is there a chance for me?"

Rigo carried on staring, no one could have guessed what was going through his mind, His face was blank and he was staring at me like it was the first time he was seeing me. He looked at my hands and then back to my eyes and smiled broadly.

"You sound like a teenager bro!" he started laughing, closing his eyes and rocking back. "You really do care don't you?" I nodded and he took a long pause “You recognise that when God made her He broke the mould. I never met another girl like her and to have her as a sister I know I am blessed and the world will be well if she is around” he leaned back on his hands in the sand and smiled again. “I tell you what I know Marcus, ok, seriously, and I hope you listen because deep down I am happy she found you. You are a great guy dude, you have been super good to the kids and even Nana. Honestly bro, from my heart thank you. Maybe this might offend you but I didn’t expect you to be so old you know, I didn’t expect you to be so chill. I thought you would still be about the girls, parties and all of that but I was totally wrong. I agree with you, it feels like we have known you forever and to be honest that’ll be the part of all of this that scares Sol the most. She doesn’t like to share herself with people, she doesn’t like to talk about the past and her upbringing. She had it rough dude, she was mostly homeless until her and Brody managed to get a little piece of shit by the sea” he said quite honestly, but then checking himself on his opinion. “Don’t ever tell her I said that, she thinks that place was a castle by the way” he paused and winked at me.

"Nah, you want too much from her bro, you want to know her inside and out and you can't ever do that. She is an enigma but she is honest and legit. You will always know what she thinks if you care enough to ask, you will always get a straight opinion regardless if it hurts and if she loves you back, ah now there bro, you hit the jackpot. She loves with her whole heart, she loves with a fierce passion and will stay loyal to you forever. So you ask yourself this Marcus, would you be able to handle it if by some miracle she loved you back, she chose to give you a chance?" he asked, searching my face and feeling comforted enough to continue.

"I doubt she would ever be by your side professionally; you know in front of the camera and shit cause that is not her scene but she would be waiting for you when you got home and she would brighten up every day of your life. You think you can safeguard that kind of treasure bro, you think you are man enough to go on such an intense journey? You mess her around and not only will the entire barrio come fuck you up but karma seems to have a nasty way of dealing with those who aggrieve her. I would be happy to see her get a life she deserves. You could take her travelling, exploring, teach her new things, help her with her work and give her a taste of the good life right? And that makes me happy but you have to think of the kids too Marcus, they come too. She is a fierce tiger mama when it comes to them, she always had to be but you know they come too. So before you unleash some fantasy romance that may or may not last a lifetime think about all of that. You would go from single, rock super star living la vida loca to dad of two and loyal partner to one woman, all a bit new to you right?" he asked knowingly, looking slightly smug, but I knew he was speaking the truth.

I nodded yes but actually everything he was saying was true. Funny thing was I wanted all that, la vida loca, far from it! I was living alone, no one to sit with in the evenings, I toured on my own and slept on my own, ate on my own and just seemed to spend a lot of time on my own. Yes, I could go wherever I wanted and I could do whatever I wanted but I was tired of that life now. Having an angel waiting for me to come home, having the kids come on tour with all the other kids with us, just doing normal things with a family. Maybe it was time to make an instant family and take a big leap. I was still confused though, I knew I wanted to be with her in any capacity she would allow but would she give me that chance?

"Rigo, how can I make her stay? How can I ask her to give me a chance? I want all of that, honestly. When I held her today I knew it was right, we could be together forever like that, it was just so perfect, so natural. Please help me bro, I promise I will never hurt her, never her, never the kids. Tell me what to do, please" the words tumbled out before I could control them and sounded almost pathetic and lovelorn. I just knew having her stay was what I really wanted and I had suddenly demonstrated how much I truly cared for Soleil. She had come into my life many times before but this time came at the right time; not just for me but for her. I was ready to take on children and responsibilities because I realised how much you get back from it all. But the ball was in her court, it was her move next, I had no control over the next steps because I knew I had to respect this marvel and allow it to be according to its own laws of existence.

Rigo looked at me and lit his joint up again, he wasn't going to rush this, he knew it was important to get it right. He exhaled some rings and looked back out over the sea.

"You need to perfect your emotions towards her and the kids, you need to understand them. The kids come first, if they want to stay, Sol will seriously consider it if they don't she is gone. Just sit back and let the universe come to you and present its gifts. Just stay calm and quiet, let what is written be spelled out. You will soon see you do not need to do anything except exactly what you were doing before. Relax bro, smoke a bit more, your boy Gordo sends his love." Rigo blew me a kiss and winked then laughed at his own joke. "Seriously, relax Marcus, stress doesn't suit you, makes you look old." He chuckled.

"You are funny when you are fucked up Rigo, fucking hilarious" I grabbed the remainder of the spliff and took a drag. Rigo was right; I was an open book, unashamedly showing my feelings and deepest desires to the world. Let's see what comes back to me. I looked over at Rigo, he looked super pleased and like he was about to take a nap. I stared out to sea again and waited like a slow cheetah to see what the day would bring.

She hadn't come back that day but I knew she wasn't when we got back about an hour later and Nana said she had spoken to her, they were at Disneyland. That was the last place I thought she would go but I guess for the kids it made sense.

Nana and Rigo packed up the car and left, Rigo, gave me a big bear hug when he left and reminded me to think about what I really wanted from all this and promised to let me know how they were doing.

I finished making my tea and walked outside. I had so many scenarios playing in my mind. What did I have left to give, where would I find the capacity to continue and produce the work of life and rhythm that had been the soundtrack to my life thus far. I sipped my tea and looked out over the cliffs, if you stood here you could not see the bottom and the beach, you knew it was there but you could not see it. Like life, you knew the treasures and delights of this world awaited you just had to believe that; because if life sweeps you up in a torrent wind and hurls you over the cliff, you will feel helpless, you will feel change all about you as you tumble and wrench around the sky; but you will also cling to what you know, what you know is promised you and perhaps the wind will die down and gently place you down on the sandy beach in the sun or continue to blow you out to sea, on to another struggle which ultimately will guide you back to firm ground after struggle and the relief and gratefulness will return and humble you to your core and make you see what is truly important. I knew I could carry on for another twenty-five in the same way, it was a good life and I was grateful always. I had been humbled so many times in my life I knew better, but if she came back and the whirl of the wind ignited the push pull, perhaps there was a new struggle or a perfect beach that awaited but whatever it was I knew I had enough inside me to give much and take very little, laughter, joy and life held a higher value to me now.

CHAPTER TWENTY

I decided it was best to stay away another night at the beach hut after all that had happened yesterday at the office. After receiving the reaction that I did I thought it best to give myself and Marcus some more room as I didn't really want to feel accountable for my work or my decisions just yet. The hotel was available so I paid for another night and we planned another fabulous and well deserved beach day with Nana for the morning. Rigo had to go get the van ready for a radio show he was catering for the next day and wanted to prep as much as he could so he decided to leave after breakfast.

"You know you owe me some hours Sol, seriously, you was meant to be working the van with me sis. You think you all big now cause you going to live in some rock star mansion!" he threw in thinking he was funny. I glared at him and put down my coffee ready to let loose.

"Mija, shh, stupid boy. Rodrigo! Go home and do some work. She is on vacation and we are going to enjoy some peace and quiet now so go!" she shushed him and waved him out the door.

I took a deep breath and calmed down, as usual Nana was right and I wanted to really enjoy today and relax. I had to figure out the next step. Lily already asked if we were going 'home' tonight. I gathered them together and asked the kids what they wanted to do. I told them Marcus had said we could stay but that we also had enough money now to get our own place by the sea. It wouldn't have a pool or be as big but it would be just them and Nana when she could visit. I left them with Nana for a few hours and went for a swim in the sea, I wanted them to think about their answer because it meant and awful lot to me and would help me see our best way forward. I spread out on my back and glided like silk over the waves. The sun was bright and invigorating, I wondered if Marcus was out to sea again, searching for the same calm as me and unafraid of its embrace and journey. I knew what the kids would say and I knew we would go back to his home to find our future and I felt strong enough to restrict myself this time, to not give so much of me. I was worn and needed repair, the band would tour soon and perhaps if we stayed we would have some time together to process all that had happened and really experience the option we had been gifted and maybe Marcus would not be a constant anyway as he would have to go tour sooner or later.

I sat down soaking into the warm and sparkling sand, the waves were crashing onto the beach and the cycle continued, never stopping. I wanted to be the wave now, not the beach. I had absorbed life enough for three and now I wanted to crest and break and be cradled back out to sea and lifted to new shores. I knew my stubbornness and deep insecurities would hinder me along the way and force me to consciously unfix my feet and ride away, but maybe it was time to trust again and believe. No one was complaining and no one was exasperated, we had managed to come together and feel welcome and relaxed. It all felt so normal and recognizable; but I knew if we stepped back into the house something will have changed. For a start I am sure I had been exposed professionally, so he knew I had been working on that very film inside his own home, secondly we both knew we were drawn together and shared a kindred awakening inside. It was this that scared me because I knew there was a huge amount of emotion, unanswered questions and discovery that awaited us, we were both curious to know if we were suited, mated or even compatible. Something told us we were, and his embrace, his warm gentle arms around me; I knew something powerful lurked there and was either the best thing that could happen next or another disaster slowly gaining momentum until it plays itself deep within and then unleashes its full force and inertia. Whatever I felt, I knew it was powerful and intrinsic; I was drawn back to the house, back to the man.

I got up and went back to the kids and Nana who had set up their towels and umbrella further up the shore. A wave of relief swept over me when I saw them the fear and distress was gone and they looked relaxed and just normal again. Nothing had been easy to understand or straightforward for any of them but they had trusted me and had faith in what I was doing. Fortune had smiled fondly upon us and then taken away my biggest love and fear all at the same time. We had a home to go to that was warm, exciting and secure, no storms seemed to rock the walls and no sirens or shots resounded in your subconscious as you slept. There was a chance for everyone to strive and do better, seek new adventures and get as much love and happiness out of life possible.

“Hey ma, how was the swim?” Lily asked brightly, breaking away from her sand spires that adorned her sand castle.

“Great baby, how is your castle coming along? When do we move in?” I joked back.

“We don’t need to move in Ma, we decided we like Marcus’ house and we miss Dani so if it is still okay we would like to go back there. But we want to unpack some more of our stuff because we are missing a few important pieces to our Monopoly game!” Lily said with a bright smile like she had just announced the agreement of world peace. I was slightly taken aback by her assuredness but I smiled knowing deep down I was happy this would be the path we took and that we could return to such a beautiful home and such kind people. I turned to look at Nana as I knew she had heard that and she looked stern and nodded towards Jason. He was sitting slightly away from them on the sand, absentmindedly flicking sand with a small red spade. He was staring out to sea and had a very pensive look on his face. His hair was getting long and was blowing in the wind like a like golden fleece and he looked almost fearless yet so innocent all at once. My heart pulled towards him but I knew he needed some space too, he was like his dad in that respect, he needed to think on things before he decided what was best. He was a listener and a learner; he paid attention to the world around him and sought the knowledge he needed to make sure his next step was comfortable and considered. This was what Brody had lost; his mind made him restless and the drugs soothed and slowed his rhythm so he could just exist at times. Jason was just far more creative and a master of lateral thinking, often stating the clearest fact and always marvelling at the elephant in the room. I walked closer to him and sat down facing the same direction and looking out over the sea. A small fishing boat was setting out a small net about a quarter of a mile out to sea, the boat was steady as the sea was pretty calm that day but the beauty was the birds that were circling above seeking scraps of bait disappearing under the water. They did figure eights and dives, making a normal day of fishing seem like a ballet from those watching from afar. We sat and watched for a while and when the net had finally been cast the birds lost interest and each took flight in a different direction meeting higher in the skies, reforming their flock and disappearing. Jason stood up and moved closer to me, plopping himself down next to my knee. He rested his arms on my leg and looked up at me with no intention of speaking yet, just making sure he had my attention. I brushed the golden threads from his face and bent over him to kiss his sweet head; I took his face in my hands and said "Tell me my young journeyman, what did you see just now?" in my most regal tone.

"Just birds trying to steal the bait ma, they are just trying to get a cheap meal, but I love to watch the way they fly. They move all over, never bumping in to each other and then they might leave separately but they find each other again and move on together. I would love to fly, but then I guess you three would have to learn too because otherwise we couldn't find each other again and move on. Right ma?" he responded matter of factly.

"You are totally right J, but I wouldn't mind flying so you can count me in and I am sure if I do it then Lil will too. Problem is Nana and Rigo you see, they don't fly. Never have!" I laughed thinking of the last time I suggested flying to San Francisco.

"Do you think Marcus wants to fly ma?" he asked suddenly and made me stop and look him straight in the eyes. They were very curious and questioning, he brought up the obvious topic he knew we had to discuss and he wanted information.

"You know J, I don't really know" I began "You see, I am a little confused on what we should do, but what I do know is I want your honest opinion now because we have to make a choice and we have to all agree to either fly or stay grounded. I know it might seem like a big deal but know this, we are going to stick together and whatever you and Lily want to do is what we will try. I don't know what the future looks like anymore but I know we will always be together wherever we go." I stroked his hair and looked at his face lovingly.

He looked up at me and took his time to begin, "So Lily wants to go back to Marcus' house and I sort of do too because I miss Dani and the pool. Thing is ma, I think I miss Marcus too. He is pretty cool and he knows a lot of stuff and gets to see lots of cool things all over the world. But that is also what makes me sad because we lost dad now too and Marcus isn't my dad but I kind of want him to be now. Is that mean? Would pa be mad at me for saying that?"

"No, no Jason, not at all!" I quickly responded "No, J, he would be happy you are not sad and he would be happy you are safe and not missing him too much. The thing is Jason, he is a good guy, you are right, but who knows how we will all feel six months from now. Maybe you won't like it there anymore and I want you to know that is okay too. We are going to go day by day and just enjoy the blessings around us. You know, we have to go back to doing normal things too, the summer is nearly over!" I added.

"Ya, I see what you mean. I like that better anyways. It's nice to just enjoy the day and the things you get to see every day. Lily will be happy and I think you will too ma, we will go to the beach every day and you can swim and look for treasures with me. We could learn how to sail a boat and then maybe go fishing and things like that. It will be fun, I trust you ma, and if you trust Marcus then so do I" he pledged solemnly.

"Okay, then I guess it is settled now, tonight we go back to Malibu and see what adventure awaits us!" I grabbed him up and rolled in the sand with him tickling his sides and laughing along with him. My little imp was full of life and spirit that I never wanted to see extinguished and full of the thirst for life that would only be quenched by adventure and risk. I was looking forward to our bold step ahead and I felt more blessed than ever with the gift of such purity and loyalty gifted onto me in such a marvellous form. Both of them; jewels, always sparkling and delighting the eye of those that love them most. We stopped rolling and raced towards Nana and Lily who were opening up the picnic basket.

"I am starving Nana, give me everything you got!" Jason shouted still full of glee and delight.

"Music to my ears! Amen!" Nana sang. We all fell into laughter and started passing around the delights of Nana's picnic basket. "So what is this I hear about you people staying in Malibu?" Nana broke the silence and asked sternly but then breaking into a smile and putting her arm around Jason. "I am happy you have chosen this ninos, very happy."

"You will visit right Nana and stay the night too?!" Jason pleaded.

"Of course I will! With your mom's cooking ability being zero I need to come rescues your tummy's don't I?!" she joked back.

I leaned over towards Nana and threw my arms around her and held her tightly. "Gracias Nana, thank you, God Bless you always" I whispered into her neck comforted she heard me by the tightening of her arms around me and I felt her breath catch as she kissed my head. I held on to her and felt calm, the kids got up and joined in the huddle. We said nothing but felt much and told each other how much we loved one another and how blessed we were to have found each other and survived the worst. We all had hope, whether for ourselves or for each other and this would fuel us and clear the path of negativity and darkness. We saw light in each other and in the future, we basked under the sun but radiated from the inside because what we knew was what we had, what came next came at us together, forever.

CHAPTER TWENTY-ONE

We pulled up to the house in the evening, the kids were tired but excited to get back and set some ownership up over the place as they planned to really explore this option and see what lay in store. It was a world away from anything we could have ever dreamed of but this was also why it was so attractive; it was a dream, for a child what more could you ask for, Malibu was a fantastic place to be a kid. I was quiet most of the way there as I had no idea what would happen if Marcus was home. I had no idea what he had been through in the last few days, I had seen him of course but that was my choice. I left the house after a night of enchantment darkened by fear as the clouds followed the sunrise, I could not see any other way, so much had happened in such a short space of time. He was awakened to the wounds I had suffered and had a glimpse of what I had survived; this on top of finding me exposed, out to sea, just in case he didn't think I was crazy enough. However, a genuine request to stay and a warm and welcome invitation to do just that had been expressed, mutually, and I was willing to take a chance on that and give the kids the chance to enjoy a life beyond anything I could have imagined or provided. This was their payback for being strong during the storms and getting help that ultimately saved us all.

I was sure something would have signalled our arrival but it was only when I put the key in the door we heard Dani bark excitedly.

“Be careful kids, she must have missed you so much!” I said with a huge grin, I had missed Dani too she was great to have at the beach and Jason adored her.

I opened the door and sure enough Dani was barely two feet away barking and leaping up, tail wagging as fast as a hummingbird’s wing! “Dani!” they shouted in unison and ran towards their four-legged friend. Dani was so excited she didn’t know who to snuzzle first. “Aw we missed you so much girl, we have so much to tell you about Disneyland!” Lily squealed and Dani licked her cheek.

“Hey Dani” I called, “Where is your daddy, girl?” She broke away from the kids and came over to me and I bent down to tussle her head and give her a stroke. It felt like no one was home, but I had seen two bikes parked outside so I knew Marcus was home. It suddenly struck me that he might have company, like company he didn't want us to be a part of kind of company. I was suddenly filled with dread; I had made my choice but I had not sought to even see if the offer still stood and if we were welcome. What if I had just walked in on a situation that was unwelcome and could lead to a confrontation in front of the kids. I had taken for granted the feelings of security and warmth without considering what the impact of leaving that morning would have had on Marcus. Maybe he had changed his mind and having us here was no longer a desire or favor. I only had one choice, I had to get an answer, understand what the next step was and move. Survival mode kicked in and I stood up, "Stay here with Dani guys, let me see if anyone is home" I called behind me as I walked towards the kitchen as all of the lights were on, hoping I was wrong but having no idea what to expect. Dani went back to the kids and they were soon back to giggling and telling her all about their last few days.

As I reached the island in the middle of the kitchen, I looked outside, standing next to the pool was Willow and Marcus, the doors were shut and I guess they didn't hear Dani barking; but one look at Marcus' face and I could see that they were in a deep conversation and just completely unaware of the world around their words. Willow walked over to Marcus and put his big arm around his shoulders and tousled his hair, his six foot plus frame looking protective next to Marcus who looked slumped and so small all of a sudden. I watched this bond admiringly and with familiarity, these two had been together since high school, life had rocked them from left to right and up and down. They had survived these last twenty-five years because they held on to the original high; the music, the fans, the journey. I am not sure how long I watched for, they started talking again and out of nowhere Jason ran past me and straight towards the patio door. Willow caught sight of a flash of color and slapped Marcus on the back saying something with a huge smile. Jason reached the door as Marcus turned and caught sight of him; Jason flung open the door and ran straight towards both men.

"Marcus! We're home!" Jason shouted as he flew into his chest and threw his little arms around him as tight as he could. Marcus looked like he was in shock as he realized what he had just said and quickly broke out into a huge grin and hugged Jason right back. Willow was stood next to them and he looked into the kitchen and smiled. I locked eyes with him and smiled back, appreciative of the warmth and genuineness he exuded. Lily came running past with Dani in tow having heard Jason locate Marcus.

"Marcus! Marcus, we have so much to tell you!" Lily shouted in delight as she locked eyes on Marcus, who was still hugging Jason. He looked up and when he saw Lily his eyes brightened even more and he held out one arm for her to join in.

"Does this mean you are staying a little while then?" he asked them brightly but wanting to know this was not just a visit and slightly taken aback.

"We decided we wanted to come back Marcus and stay if that is still okay. We love it here and you are like the best uncle we could have ever dreamed of. This is like a dream come true, ten times better than Disneyland... Except Space Mountain, that was pretty cool" Jason concluded with a firm nod of his head and looking Marcus straight in the eye.

"Ya that was so cool, but Ma said it was up to us and we want to give this a try. Ma is here too! She is still in the kitchen!" Lily added, always happy to have the last word. They all looked towards the kitchen and I was spotted. I waved stupidly towards them and smiled.

“Hey Kids! Where have you been? Did you say Disneyland?!” Willow asked his deep voice booming through to the kitchen.

“Hi Willow! We did, we went to Disneyland!” Lily answered with a smile, “It is nice to see you again, did you come to play volleyball with us again?”

Marcus had released the kids as they wanted to say hello to Willow and they grabbed Willow’s hands and started walking towards the pool already chatting a million miles an hour about their celebrity encounters at Disneyland. Marcus’ eyes stared through to the kitchen door as he stood up; I watched him as I slowly lifted my eyes to meet his. I knew my eyes betrayed me and told him how pleased I was to see him and the relief that calmed my heart slightly. He smiled and began to walk towards me and I stood still, suddenly hoping the island would stay between us right now as being close to him would distract me and prevent me understanding what our return actually meant to him. He came inside and stood on the other side of the island, still respecting my privacy and indicating peace, not wanting me to take flight for any reason. He looked deep into my eyes and spoke softly.

"Hello Soleil, I hope you are okay? I am happy you are back, I missed you... all of you" he said in all seriousness, his mischievous twinkle muted behind his quizzical eyes. I swallowed deeply and tried to supress the nervousness I was feeling, I didn't understand where it was coming from but it tickled the back of my throat and the smile that would not leave my face made speaking feel impossible.

"Evening Marcus, I am good thank you. How are you? Have you been ok?" I asked trying to seem confident but most likely failing.

"Are you coming back to stay, Soleil? Are you going to give it a try?" he asked abruptly, he needed to know what was next more than I did, I suddenly realized he had not had the benefit of reflection in the same manner and was probably slightly out of his mind wanting to know where we would end up because he knew nothing about us and our resources past Nana and Rigo, he had nothing to consider because he did not know what we would do next as we had been an unexpected surprise on his door step so he knew I was mad enough to try anything to survive. I took a few deep breaths before I answered, appreciating the true importance of this moment.

"Marcus, I would really appreciate it if you would let us stay. I am not sure for how long, you see, I told the kids anytime they don't like it anymore we can move on, but for now there is really nowhere else we would like to be; and I thank you, I thank you from the bottom of my heart for giving us such an amazing opportunity to live a life we never would have known exists. So yes, we will stay if that is okay, but that is what we start with, that is what we give a try. Marcus, you have been so kind, so generous too but I am so tired, I am fragile and unbreakable all at the same time. I am not sure what I need right now, but this feels good so I will try. I will try to let you in and try to show you what the world looks like from inside here" I said tapping my head, "you see the life I lived is stubborn and will not hide away and disappear from who I am."

He looked at me from across the island and placed his hands spread open with his palms up on the counter top, "But it will fade and happiness will help the light you have shine forth again. Soleil, let me try, let me work at figuring out the complicated stuff and you just take this chance and transform your life. Let me try to help you find safety and respect, after seeing your film and your song you have mine! Let me make you and the kids laugh again and explore the world as you wish, I have the benefit of experience and that makes one patient you see, I am in no rush for anything, I am just grateful for what each day brings me. I know this sounds so profound and demanding but it is not. I stand here, the other side of an island, symbolic of the gulf I will keep and fill with respect and kindness until slowly maybe we will walk side by side. You have my respect Soleil, my utmost respect. You have survived what I only imagine and put to music, pain, fear, loss the trials you have conquered are inspiring." He finished wistfully still keeping his palms symbolically open on the counter top; contrasting against the brilliant white.

I could not respond I was thunderstruck, what was I hearing? Waves of relief washed over me and prevented any sound being omitted; I felt reassured suddenly, we had made the right decision and this was the best place we could be right now. I knew this, deep down I knew this. As if he read my mind he spoke again.

"Neither of us knows in what capacity it was meant to be, but we know deep down that fate has left us to live life alongside each other and walk a similar path. Fate has brought us all together for a time now and although fate tried before, this time the conditions are perfect and we are both at a place where we are comfortable with it and the possible future" he said knowingly and with confidence.

"I couldn't agree more Marcus, I am slightly worried about all the things we don't know but it will be nice to not have to be alone on this path, a relief in fact" I looked down at my arms that were crossed and hugging my arms at the same time. I took a deep breath and looked up, unfolding my arms and placing my finger tips on the counter with my palms dangling off. I was ready to open up and explore what felt right and recover myself and relearn what was important whilst taking in the beauty that was returning to my life. I held his gaze and eased into his stare, so much lie beneath our hands; we touched each other through the cold granite and sent warmth and willingness through its veins, connecting us, completing the circle.

A spark returned to his face and reignited the mischievous light in his eyes. "I am happy to hear that, really happy. Thank you Soleil, thank you for coming here, for taking a huge risk and for bringing Jason and Lily into my life and making this chance at happiness possible" he said sincerely turning his hands down onto the counter. I stared at his hands and felt a pull, I started to walk around the island towards him, and he looked startled by my sudden bold movements but instinctively he walked around towards me, meeting me more than halfway. "I will take two steps for every one that you take, I will be here for you, I promise" he held out his hand hopefully. I immediately took it in both of mine and held it close to my chest.

"I am scared Marcus, that is the truth. I don't know how this will work and I don't know anything about being a celebrity in this world. I trust you but I don't trust myself I guess" I blurted out, my face a show of worry. I wanted to be more confident and fearless but I had nearly lost myself on a bad judgment, I could not risk all I had left.

"Please, trust me Soleil, we will figure it out. First we get you back to your best, then we start when you are ready. Let's get the kids settled again and if they want to unpack their stuff that would be cool too. Willow stayed last night but he used Nana's room so your rooms are as you left them." He said coolly trying to normalize my fears and be practical but with concern and earnest care in his face.

“Nana has a room?!” Suddenly I burst out laughing, I lifted his hand to my mouth as I could not contain my laughter. This was all I needed to hear, I had all I needed and I knew life had finally swung my way. Marcus joined in with his low chuckle and I calmed down to just a chortle. I grabbed his eyes with mine again, “Don’t let me become a stress bag okay, I know we will be alright, it all just feels right” I lifted his hand to my lips and kissed his fingers, lingering, entrusting and letting him know I was sincere, never taking my eyes off his, silently thanking him and confirming my commitment to this journey. I returned his hand to my chest and stared at him, “Let’s go see what the kids are up to, once they go to sleep, let’s have that cup of tea outside by the pool” I offered.

He squeezed my hands from inside their grasp and placed his other hand on mine. A solid connection was formed and the circle was complete for sure now. “Sounds perfect Soleil, let’s go see what is next.”

Printed in Great Britain
by Amazon

13969261R00178